The Lion's Mouth

A Nick Lawrence Novel: Book 2

By
Brian Christopher Shea

Acclaim for Shea's first novel, The Camel's Back

"THE CAMEL'S BACK took me on a journey of loss, heartache, resilience and triumph experienced by the characters. Reading it opened my eyes to the hardships law enforcement officials face and gave me a deeper respect for and gratitude to the heroes who risk their lives to protect us every day. Brian Shea also humanized an often stereotyped figure and allowed me to dive into the antagonist's mind and understand what drove him to his fateful decisions. Brian's background in law enforcement gives the well-researched book authenticity. I look forward to reading more of this series."
- Charlotte Kovalchuk, The Williamson County Sun

"Shea's novel is quick-moving, exciting, and eventful...The lingo and parlance of the military/law enforcement characters read smoothly. Readers will be interested in the behind-the-scenes aspect of the fast-paced military operations...Shea's portrayal of Declan Enright is solid and realistic..."
- The BookLife Prize

Readers' Opinions Matter:

Wow. This was a fascinating read. Not usually into books about FBI but this one caught my attention and kept me turning page past midnight last night. If this is Mr. Shea's first book, he has a great career ahead of him.
Betty (Goodreads Review)

The Camel's Back story brings you right along with the well-developed characters and, even though it's extremely driven by action sequences, each of the characters have complexities that create emotional attachment for the reader. I don't want to give too much away, but there is one character whose archetype is often painted with a broad brush. Shea's treatment of this character humanizes and "ups" the stakes for all involved.
Greg (Amazon Review)

The author, Brian Shea, has touched a raw nerve with this book and should be commended for attempting to critique our values, our material progress and our interconnectedness as all human being sharing this planet. The world is no longer black and white and this book shines a brighter light than most, to reveal the underbelly of society we live in. Kudos on the first novel and looking forward to the second and third novels.
Zara13 (Amazon Review)

It made me get up and make sure my doors were locked. The action scenes were very well done, at times I had to cover the bottom of the page while reading the top!
Colleen (Goodreads Review)

With an artful blend of thoughtful narration and deeply developed characters, Brian Christopher Shea expertly weaves together a complex storyline that not only blurs the line between right and wrong - It totally annihilates it with a plot arc so captivating it's truly hard to put the book down.
Steve (Amazon Review)

Once I started I was hooked on the unpredictable story line, and could not put it down. The intermingled lives of these relatable characters operating in the gray zone called life, capture the genuine family struggles for those who run towards the gunfire or wear the stars facing forward. This is not a book to read once and never pick up again – it is a conversation starter.
Heather (Goodreads Review)

What the Experts are Saying:

The Lion's Mouth

A Nick Lawrence
Novel: Book 2

By
Brian Christopher
Shea

ISBN: 9781983313462

Author Photograph by Adam Rembisz

Proofreading by Daniel:
https://www.fiverr.com/mrproofreading

Cover design by Vikki Davies
www.fiverr.com/vikncharlie

Back cover photo of Shane Murphy's K9 "Marley" by Joe Muaro.

Dedication

This book is dedicated to the taken. To those children swallowed by the beast that is human trafficking. Keep your strength and stay in the fight. Know that there are good people out there looking for you and hunting those responsible.

Chapter 1

It was the sound that woke her. The rumble of the truck's tires as they slowly veered off the roadway and into the breakdown lane. The stagnant air was ripe. She assumed that it must be night or early morning. Her exposed leg was pressed up against the metallic wall of the box truck and it was not warm. It had been hot earlier. Almost burning her skin.

She could hear the muffled voices of the two men in the cab of the truck. *Why are we stopping?* The last time it was bad. This time could be worse. They had taken an interest in her. She knew the interest from men like this was never good.

Death has a unique smell. Mouse was not unaccustomed to it but, in the enclosed space of the truck, it sickened her. He'd been dead for over a day. The humidity didn't allow for his blood-soaked shirt to dry. Mouse could feel the moistness of it dampen hers. She managed to shift the weight of the lifeless man off her but could not completely separate from him. Too many people. Too little space. His bowels had released. That smell had intertwined with the others who had turned the 6x14 foot living space into a toilet on wheels. Mouse had urinated in her pants too many times to count, but they were beginning to dry now that dehydration had set in. She'd hoped that the smell of her urine-soaked clothing would deter the two men in the front from their intentions.

The last time the truck pulled off the road they had already been riding for a while, but time was an elusive thing under the circumstances. The door had swung open. It was still dark, but Mouse had been able to see a hint of light in the background. Though she was unable to determine if the sun was rising or setting. Everyone stirred when the truck door opened. Any hope that the long journey was over quickly dissipated. The fat man had grabbed Mouse's leg and began pulling her out toward the opening. The thin man stood beside his fat friend. His long greasy hair slicked back with sweat. His eyes were wild. Mouse feared him most. The thin man started to unzip his faded dirt-covered jeans. The old man realized what was happening. He tried to protect her. He had smacked the hand of the fat man with a scar over his left eye. A mistake.

The thin man withdrew a large knife from a worn leather sheath that hung from his sagging pants. The sound of the knife plunging in and out of the old man was a sound that Mouse never wanted to hear again. Pop and thud. Pop and thud. The old man never screamed. He whimpered softly in sync with the plunge of the blade. Each sound softer than its predecessor until the old man slumped over and onto Mouse. The thin man smiled and zipped his pants. His primal needs satiated. The fat man retracted and closed the door. Darkness again. A few of the others sobbed quietly at what they had just witnessed. Mouse had not.

That was yesterday, or what felt like yesterday. This time would be different. There was no kind-hearted old man to save her. She would have to fend for herself. Her father had long ago prepared her for this journey, for the potential gauntlet she'd face. And he'd prepared her well. The men in the cab of the truck would underestimate her. Her small size had earned her the nickname. But she knew that *Big things come in small packages*.

Mouse could hear the two outside. The harshness of their voices muffled by the heavy doors. Then laughter. An unsettling sound. It did little to belie their true intention. *Focus. Visualize what you need to do. Commit to the action needed. Then act.* Her father's simple words replayed in her head as they had a thousand times before. She had proven the value of their meaning and this would be yet another test.

The padlock attached to the latch stirred. In the darkness, she edged closer to the door. The grunts of the others as she crawled over them seemed louder in the silence. There were men, women and children of all ages huddled together in the truck's dark interior. They were unknowingly sold into servitude with the promise of reaching America. Each of her cabin mates destined for different services. There were whispers among the imprisoned that the younger women and children would undoubtedly end up in the sex trade. The older men and women would be put to work in sweatshops or as day laborers. The desperation of their circumstance seemed to drain their will to fight back. Not Mouse. It fueled a fire inside her.

She'd reached her destination, feeling the cool metal of the double doors. Mouse rolled silently onto her back. Her head rested against the back of one of the others. It would give her added leverage when the time came. Mouse's feet rose high and the soles of her worn sneakers now rested lightly against the door. *Commit to the action needed.*

The clank of the hinge told her that the time had come. The tension in the doors released and they swung wide. The darkness of the sky seemed bright against the pitch of the box truck's interior. *Act.*

Mouse shot her feet outward, striking at the two men. Her back arched on impact as they found their intended targets, one foot connecting with each man's throat. *Big things CAN come in size 5 shoes.* A gurgling cough erupted from the fat man. The thin man was quiet. As Mouse sat up she understood why. His eyes were wild but not like the day before. This was fear. A palpable terror on the man's bony face. His hands clasped tightly around his throat. A horrible wheezing sound expelled from his crushed windpipe as he staggered backward. The thin man fell and rolled into the shallow ditch that ran alongside the road. His body continued to writhe in agony, twisting to avoid the end that was fast approaching.

The fat man was not down. He was recovering from the initial blow, but his hands no longer held near his throat. His body hunched and his hands on his knees. Mouse had planned for the possibility that the fight wouldn't be over with one action.

Earlier, she had taken the tattered leather belt from the old man and now it was wrapped tightly around her right hand. Even in death, he would protect her one last time. The oversized belt buckle was exposed across her knuckles. The image embossed in the steel depicted a cowboy on a bronco. Apropos in the desert landscape of this standoff.

Mouse slipped out and onto the roadway. Her legs momentarily unsteady, adjusting as she stood for the first time after the long confinement. The fat man did not notice her. He was loud, spitting and cursing. She swung upward hard. Again, she found her target. The trachea. This time with the added devastation of the buckle. The blow sent his head straight up. Bewildered, the fat man tried to account for this new injection of pain. His hands were back at his throat. *Remember, Mouse, no matter how big your enemy, the throat is weak.* Her dad's words. Wise and true.

The fat man dropped to his knees. The jagged scar above his eye seemed more menacing in his current state. Fearful that he would recover and overpower her, Mouse moved quickly, timing her next assault.

The belt hung loosely in her hand as she shot behind the fat man. His hands lowered as he went to all fours, trying to find her like a dog chasing his tail. The leather strap wrapped around his throat. Mouse quickly slid the open end through the buckle and pulled it taut. A make-shift choke collar. Mouse was airborne. Her knees landed squarely in the fat man's back, toppling him face-first into the asphalt. Mouse now stood with the heels of her small feet rooted in his shoulders. She leaned back hard like a water skier in the wake of a speedboat.

The fat man flailed his arms, but the lack of oxygen weakened their movement. Mouse counted in her head. 6...7...8. She felt the fat man's chest sink. His arms no longer reached for her. Eight seconds without oxygen reaching the brain and a person will sleep. Mouse was not content with sleep. She couldn't afford to have this man come for her later. Survival was an ugly business. Under the circumstances, it was fortunate that Mouse learned this sad fact early on in her short fifteen years of life.

She pulled hard until her grip could no longer hold the leather of the belt that was now slick with her sweat. Mouse released, letting the strap fall from her hand. Nothing. No movement from the fat man. As morning's light began to cast its eerie glow she stared at the fat man's chest. No rise. No fall. It was done. She rummaged through the pockets of both men, taking a wad of cash from each. The sheathed knife that had been used to take the life of the old man now hung from the belt on her hipline. The same belt used to finish off the fat man. Mouse's slim waist was comparable to the old man's, thus, making it a perfect fit.

She set off in the direction that the truck had been headed. Mouse did not know where she was, but she did know that anything was better than here. She looked back just once, as the other passengers in the truck clumsily started to climb out. *What can I do to help them?* The tentative looks they sent her way assured her she was making the right decision to carry on alone. *God, save them.*

Chapter 2

"Move!" Rusty Harrison directed his frustration toward the man lagging behind him. "We've got to stay on his ass. That means you've got to keep up!"

"Jesus-I-can-barely-breathe." The voice of the slow man labored as the two ran up the hill, which was covered in shrubs and thickets.

"If you can talk then you can breathe, buttercup!" Rusty called back with a laugh.

Rusty's pace quickened and the two separated further. It was of no consequence. His real partner was relentlessly pushing on ahead of him.

Jasper head down low, swiveling back and forth as he moved across the rugged terrain. He was sure-footed, anticipating any divots or obstacles. He was unrelenting in his pursuit. And, as a result, Rusty had to be too.

Jasper stopped in his tracks but only for a moment as they crested the rise. He broke right, tugging the leather strap of the leash, urging Rusty onward.

Rusty's eyes strained to adjust as dawn began to break. Light filtered in slowly and he could begin to make out the details of his surroundings. This was the first time that he was able to do this since the track began, over three miles back. Longer than most dogs could hold a scent. But Jasper wasn't most dogs.

Rusty could barely hear the labored breathing of Officer Fontaine as he worked in vain to keep up. Rusty was used to being separated and alone on a track. Fontaine wasn't the first who couldn't hang. And he wouldn't be the last. Rusty's frustration came because he now had to have his gun out while trying to navigate the uneven landscape and simultaneously manage his partner's leash. Not the best shooting platform if the situation dictated. The other problem was that Rusty's radio was set to the County channel and not the agency's that he was assisting. Essentially, Fontaine's inability to keep up had isolated them in the Texas woodland with a bad guy. A desperate and armed bad guy.

Jasper stopped again. His head lifted and cocked to one side. The brown and black ear on the right side of his head flickered. Rusty had seen his partner make this gesture countless times and knew, with certainty, that this early morning track was about to come to an end.

Then Rusty heard it. The rustle of dry brush. It could have been an animal, but Jasper didn't care about such things. At least not while on the hunt. His focus was unparalleled to other dogs that Rusty had managed in the past.

Rusty released the leash's clasp connected to the collar. Free from restraint, Jasper stilled his body.

Waiting. Rusty slowed his breathing. Then he heard the distinct sound, the clink of a metal object on stone. Gun.

Before Rusty could give Jasper the command, Fontaine bounded down the hill. He crashed through the thick ground vegetation and shouted, "Jesus! You boys sure can move. I swear to God I've never run so fa–."

The sentence was left unfinished as the shot rang out. Fontaine dove for the cover of a nearby tree. He hit the ground, flopping onto his protruding belly as he crawled for safety. Rusty stood ready and pointed his gun in the direction of where the shot originated but couldn't find the target. Jasper had.

Jasper was gone. Full throttle through underbrush, snapping branches as he moved like a torpedo through water. The land shark on attack was a beautiful thing to witness. His legs moved effortlessly over the terrain. No command was given by Rusty. Jasper reacted to the situation. Training played a part, but loyalty played a bigger one.

The man stood from behind a clump of shrubs. He was rail thin. His bony frame was readily apparent through the sweat-drenched t-shirt that clung to his body. His hair was shaved short and his face gaunt. The visible scabbing on his forehead and cheeks bore the trademark of his drug habit. Crystal methamphetamine usage was common in this part of the country where open spaces lent to clandestine laboratories, or homegrown "cooks." *Meth-head tweakers were almost always unstable. Armed ones were the worst.*

The gaunt man stumbled back as he saw Jasper closing the distance, looking for his escape. His limited brain capacity obviously struggled with the choices of running, fighting or giving up. Overwhelmed, he glanced down the hill and then back at Jasper. Eyes wide, the gaunt man raised the gun.

Jasper was airborne. As if shot from a cannon, he launched at the gaunt man. Rusty had often joked about getting his dog a red cape. He was in awe every time he saw his four-legged partner fly.

Bang! The sound was deafening in still morning air. The gun went off again as Jasper smashed headlong into the gaunt man. The two toppled over and rolled further down the hill in a blur of man and animal.

Rusty momentarily froze after the shots. Not out of any fear for his own safety but out of that for his best friend's. He suppressed this sick wave of panic that rose up inside him. Rusty ran at the two who had stopped their roll after colliding with a large tree stump.

Rusty heard what he was looking for as he ran. Screams. That almost lyrical vaulted yell that people gave as Jasper found purchase with his teeth. Jasper's jaw was stretched wide as he held on the rear of the gaunt man's upper right leg. The growling that accompanied the bite added to the Gaunt man's hysteria.

The gaunt man clawed at the ground, reaching frantically. Rusty instantly realized that this man was not only trying to escape the clasp but was also trying to find the gun. Rusty closed the last few feet quickly. The gaunt man's fingertips were outstretched, nearing the brown handle of the revolver that peeked out from under a broken tree branch. Rusty delivered a solid kick to the gaunt man's ribcage. The effect was immediate and had the desired reaction. The gaunt man's hands retracted and

Rusty positioned himself, stepping on the revolver as he pointed his Glock at the man's head.

"Get him off of me!" The gaunt man shouted. "Help! Help me!"

"Hands! Let me see your damn hands!" Rusty said, allowing his controlled anger to be released.

The kick had brought the gaunt man's hands in and away from the gun, but now they were no longer visible as he lay face down in agony. The sound of Jasper's low growl as he continued to tug at the man brought a barely noticeable smile to Rusty's face.

"He won't stop until I tell him to. Hands!" Rusty said, with composure.

The gaunt man's hands crept out between anguished screams. Empty. No weapon. Rusty held the gun steady as Fontaine clamored over, out of breath.

"Cuff him!" Rusty hissed.

Fontaine fumbled with his handcuffs. Rusty heard the click as the stainless-steel bracelets ratcheted down on the man's boney wrists. Secured. Fontaine stood and nodded at Rusty.

"Foos!" Rusty commanded. With that one word, Jasper released his grip and sat next to Rusty.

Jasper licked the blood from his lips, never taking his dark eyes off the man on the ground. With the gaunt man in custody, Rusty immediately ran his hands anxiously over his partner. He searched both by touch and sight for any sign of a gunshot wound. Nothing. The only blood was that of the gaunt man's. Rusty slumped next to his best friend and pulled him close. He let out a sigh of relief, rubbing him between the ears.

Rusty leaned close to Jasper and whispered, "Good boy, Jasper! Good boy!"

Chapter 3

"I don't understand. That'll make it two times this week alone. We've got to figure this out," Nick said, in a combination of frustration and defeat.

"Mr. Lawrence, this is actually quite typical of someone in her condition. She is in a new environment and your mother hasn't adapted to it yet. This takes time. She will have moments of confusion and lapses in judgment as a result. Her inability to recognize a familiar face or her surroundings can be devastating. Violent outbursts are very common reactions and you shouldn't be too alarmed," the doctor said, speaking clearly and slowly.

The tone of the physician's response bordered on condescending, but Nick was too absorbed in his sense of guilt that he hadn't picked up on it. *She's lashing out because she is lost*. Nick felt the burden resting heavily on his shoulders. He'd brought her out here and put her in a place that was foreign to her. She's surrounded by people that she doesn't know and now she was lashing out as a result. *His sweet frail mother was attacking people.*

"Is the nurse okay?" Nick asked, concerned for the nurse and the potential liability that may follow.

"She's fine, Mr. Lawrence. Your mother scratched her arm, but the injury was superficial," the doctor said, calmly.

"I'll be by later today to visit with her. Are you sure that you don't need me right now? I'm stuck at work but can finagle my way out if you think this circumstance dictates," Nick's response did little to hide his annoyance.

"Later will be fine. Depending on what time you arrive, I may still be here. If so, please have me paged. We need to discuss some potential changes in your mother's situation," the doctor said.

Nick understood the implication of this last comment. He took a moment to compose himself and then replied, "Doc, you just said that this was a normal reaction to her adaptation to the new environment. You told me that it's a minor incident and that the nurse was fine. What changes are you referring to?"

"We have protocols here at Pine Woods. Protocols that monitor any declines in behavior or mental state. Your mother is showing signs of both. And yes, I did say that the injury to the nurse was minor but what's not to say that the next one won't be. Earlier this week your mother shoved another resident into a wall and now we have today's incident, albeit a minor one. We have a wing here that may be more suited for her," the doctor said, speaking softly.

"Another wing? What? Like a padded room? I didn't place my mother at Pine Woods so that she could live out her remaining years in a cage," Nick let the frustration, that bubbled just beneath the surface, spill out.

The doctor took Nick's words in his stride, having heard similar sentiments before and much worse from some. He allowed a moment to pass before he continued, "I hear your frustration and I understand it. The wing that I referred to has a higher staff-to-resident ratio and your mother would no longer have a roommate. Aside from that, the accommodations would be the same."

"But I thought that was one of the benefits of your facility. I was told that having a roommate would help stimulate her and keep her more alert. Now you're telling me that she'll be in isolation?" Nick quivered; as he let the words trickle from his mouth.

"Not isolation, but more of a separation. The staff here is devout to our residents and would make sure that she is interacted with on an hourly basis." The doctor paused, hesitating briefly before he continued, "You could try to come more often, Mr. Lawrence. I don't mean to pressure you, but we discussed this seven months ago when you first came here with your mother. Your daily interaction with her is more critical to her sense of balance than you may realize. I know that you have a demanding work schedule, but you haven't been here in four days. To your mother, that's an eternity." The doctor let those last words hang in the air. They came to settle heavily on Nick's conscience.

Nick sighed. The blow delivered by the truth of the doctor's statement had landed a sucker-punch to his heart. Deflated, Nick had no steam left in his verbal repertoire to continue the banter. He conceded. "Doc, sorry for my outburst. You and your staff have been amazing. I know that I need to be there for her. I have no excuse worth giving. Hopefully, you and I can finish this conversation later this evening when I get over there."

"I look forward to it. You take care of yourself, Mr. Lawrence. And please know that your mother is in good hands here at Pine Woods," the doctor said, reassuringly.

Nick hung the phone up and slumped forward. Pressing his hand against his head, Nick stared at the sticky note on his desk. *Call Det. Jones at APD.* He took a deep breath and blew out his personal frustrations, refocusing his attention to what he did best, helping those whom could not help themselves. He thought selfishly, that it's too bad he'd never managed to apply those skills to his own life.

Chapter 4

"How many?" Nick asked, cradling his desk phone in the crux of his neck while he scribbled on a notepad.

"Seven." Detective Kemper Jones said. His voice held a slight twang, but the sharper points of his West Texas drawl had been subdued during his post-graduate work.

"Damn! Ages?"

"Eleven to sixteen," Jones spoke, matter-of-factly. It was a disconcerting aspect of the job when tragedy and trauma become commonplace.

"Do any of them speak English? Correction, are any of them speaking English?" Nick asked, knowing that Jones would understand the distinction.

Many of the people that the two investigators typically crossed paths with spoke English, but they often elected to revert to their native dialect of Spanish in the hopes that it would deter communication.

"One. Correction, one so far. The sixteen-year-old. But she's refusing to cooperate. She's been in too long," Jones said, sounding slightly put-off by the teenager.

Nick and Jones had developed a rhythm. In the short time since he'd been back in Austin, Nick crossed paths with the APD detective on several occasions. Each time the experience had been pleasurable, even if the circumstances of their encounters were not.

Each understood the other's lingo. Nick quickly grasped that the sixteen-year-old had been involved in the sex ring too long for her to give up any information about the organization. There is a loyalty, more out of a brainwashing process, that blocks long-timers from opening up about their captors. Time and patience played a huge part in getting these victims to share. The downside is that, for every minute of waiting, another girl was being added to somebody's roster.

Nick had worked several cases with Jones in the recent past and had come to respect him. His tenacity in an investigation was only rivaled by his passion for brisket. Judging by his ever-expansive midriff, Jones was amassing some serious cases lately.

"Next stop, St. David's?" Nick asked, referring to St. David's Children's Hospital in north Austin.

"Yup. I'll have two uniformed guys stay with them while we process things here," Jones said.

"Alright. Sounds like you've got things running smooth as always. I'll hang with you if that's okay?" Nick half questioned, and half stated.

"Of course. I assumed we'd be teaming up again on this one. This has obvious ties to federal jurisdiction anyway," Jones said, with no hint of sarcasm or resentment.

"I wonder if it's the same crew we went after last time," Nick said, knowing the slim likelihood of that reality.

"That'd be nice. But you know how these things go. Each case seems to hit the reset button. The demand is so high, and everyone seems to be buying in," he replied, cynicism evident; years of witnessed depravity at its root.

"Who's the room rented under?" Nick asked.

"Jose Torres. That name should be easy to track down," Jones laughed out loud at his own joke. "Probably didn't use his real name, anyway."

"True. How long were they here?" Nick knew that most of this would do little to further the investigation, but it was the standard back-and-forth.

"A week. Well, five days to be exact. Patrol showed up to investigate a noise complaint. Management said they received several calls from patrons about the volume of the television coming from the room. The patrol guys said that they could hear it through the door. When they knocked, they heard what sounded like a girl's scream. They entered with management's key and found the eleven-year-old tied to the bed. The other girls were locked in the bathroom," Jones paused only long enough to wet his dry throat with a slurp from his morning's Diet Coke, before continuing, "The perp is already being booked. A real-estate broker from Pflugerville. The guy's married with two girls about the same age. Sick bastard!"

"There's a special place in hell for assholes like him." Nick's disdain was clearly evident. "That guy is going to spend some serious time in the box with me on this. I'm going to drain every last bit of information from him."

"I would expect nothing less than your best Jedi mind tricks," Jones chuckled.

"Did he have a cell?" Nick asked.

"Yup. Snatched it. Hopefully, we get something back from digital. Sanderson is already typing the search warrant for it."

"Sounds good. I'm walking out of the building now and should be there within the next half hour or so," Nick said, ending the call as he walked into the oppressive August heat.

The weatherman had said that today's temp would be tolerable because there was going to be low humidity. *Tolerable my ass. One hundred and four degrees is hot no matter what the dew point.*

Chapter 5

The white concrete parking lot of the Stagecoach Inn was ravaged by the late afternoon sun. The layers of hot air created shimmering tendril waves of light above its surface. Nick's black Volkswagen Jetta, an asset forfeiture vehicle seized from some long-since-forgotten case, rolled to a stop behind a marked cruiser. Nick had driven the distance from his office with the windows down. He found it easier to adjust to the heat when he wasn't shut inside an air-conditioned car. It was his way of acclimating from his temperature-controlled cubicle to the outside world.

A patrolman stood talking to a maid under the minimal shade provided by the second-floor walkway. He held his notepad at the ready and jotted things down as she spoke in broken English. Sweat poured profusely from the officer's brow and he continuously swiped at it with his forearm. Nothing seemed to stop the flow. His dark uniform and twenty-plus pounds of gear did little to ease his struggle. Nick gave him a friendly nod as he passed. The patrolman returned the gesture and then quickly went back to his obligatory task of listening and sweating.

Nick ascended the metal staircase located in the center of the motel. He found the room he was looking for. It was hard to miss with three uniformed officers standing on the landing outside the open door. These were the water-cooler conversations of men and women that didn't have a traditional office. Their low-voiced discussion stopped as Nick approached.

A short officer with a bald head and ruddy cheeks turned to face Nick, obviously preparing to give the "sorry, sir, but you're going to have to go around" speech. One he'd probably given countless times since his arrival to the scene. Nick preempted this by lifting his untucked Tommy Bahama shirt to expose his badge, clipped on the right side of his hip. Nick smiled as he did this, lessening the brashness of the move.

"Detective Jones?" Nick asked, knowing that his friend was somewhere inside room 204.

"Right in here. Ummm, sir, you're going to have to sign the log," the bald officer said, with some hesitation.

"Sure thing," Nick said. He was well aware of the department's protocols about signing in and out of a crime scene on major cases. His signature was in many logbooks already and he knew, sadly, that he'd be in many more to come.

"Hey Nick, come in and check this out," Jones called out to him.

"What's up?" Nick asked as he handed the signed log to the bald officer, crossing into the room.

It was like stepping into another world. Poorly lit, even in the daylight Jones had his flashlight on. A paltry layout, furnished with a small round table, a dresser and a rickety end-table that separated the two twin beds. Nick hated that the fact that he knew why the handlers would choose a room with two beds. Double the profit. They could run two girls at the same time. One of many pieces of information that he'd wished that he'd never had reason to know.

"What do ya make of this here?"

Nick noticed that Jones's always allowed more of his West Texas accent to slip in when he worked a scene. It was like his mind was so focused on the task that he couldn't devote the extra mental resource to masking his twang.

Nick bent and examined the cheaply-made dresser and in particular the area spotlighted by Jones's flashlight. He saw the etched markings on the side closest to the bathroom wall. The spacing between the dresser and wall was small. Maybe a foot and a half gap, at best.

Los Sirvientes Del Diablo. Underneath was a crude drawing of what appeared to be a snake.

"My Spanish is coming along, but without me breaking out my phone and Googling it, then I've got no idea what it says. Well, except for devil. I got that part," Nick said, waiting for Jones to translate.

"Loosely translated, it means The Devil's Servants. Ever seen or heard it before?" Jones stood, audibly cracking his back as he righted himself.

"No. It could mean nothing. One of the girls must have wedged herself in the corner. Maybe she was just venting. Trying to separate from whatever evil was taking place at the time," Nick said.

Everything in a crime scene like this had to be evaluated for potential leads, but Nick also knew that many were dead ends. The mark of a good investigator was to eliminate those dead ends quickly so that they didn't deter from the true path. Nick wasn't just good, he excelled at this ability to differentiate. But for some reason whether it was the words or the drawing he couldn't discard it outright, yet.

"Whoever is supervising the girls have them photograph each one's hands. In particular, their fingernails."

"Okay, but why?" Jones asked, perplexed by Nick's request.

"I'm guessing none of the handlers would let these girls anywhere near a sharp object. So, this was probably done by fingernail," Nick said, softly.

"I see where you're going with this." Jones nodded his head while he spoke.

"A girl that is willing to write may be willing to talk." Nick let this settle with Jones and then continued, "You may've found the first potential lead."

"That'd be nice, but I don't think we've even come close to scratching the surface on this thing," Jones said. Too many years and too many cases prevented him from getting excited about any one clue.

"The manager said that the room was rented for the week, and that it was paid for in cash. She also said that the do not disturb sign has been up since they arrived, and no maid service was used or requested." Jones said and paused, waiting for Nick to come to the same conclusions that he already had.

"No trash? Well, that speaks volumes about this crew and the way these handlers operate. This isn't amateur hour. They've probably been cleaning up along the way. We may be hard-pressed to find anything of potential value," Nick said, letting out an exasperated sigh.

"We won't know 'til we look, but you're probably right." Jones's drawl was thick now.

"True. Very true. I wouldn't be surprised if the handler or one of their lookouts is watching the room right now. Or at least when the patrol guys arrived earlier. Whoever was running this room is definitely aware of our presence."

"Shall we divide and conquer?" Jones asked.

"Absolutely. I'd like to head to the jail and take a crack at the John who was with the eleven-year-old. Lots of ways to break a guy like that in the box. He's got a lot to lose. I'm calling dibs unless you want him?" Nick poised this to Jones, already assuming the answer.

"I wouldn't have it any other way. I'm going to stick around here for a bit and see if I can find something else to work with. Let me know as soon as you're done roasting that pervert." Jones said, giving a quick slap on Nick's right shoulder.

The shockwave from the impact sent a tingle into his arm. The pain of his repaired arm had dissipated since the explosion that had nearly torn it off, but the muscle spasms returned sporadically. All of the physical discomfort provided a constant reminder of that terrible day. But the memory was also bittersweet, a reminder of the woman that saved him. A fleeting image of Izzy drifted into his mind as he departed the room into the dazzling midmorning sun.

Chapter 6

Her small frame dragged. She stayed close to the road, using it as a guide, but worked to avoid being spotted by any of the cars and trucks that passed. Luckily, the road did not seem to be well traveled. The realization of which had begun to set in. The desolate roadway might not be as advantageous as she'd originally thought. The walk was becoming near impossible without food or water. At one point, as daylight broke behind her, she thought she saw a hamburger stacked atop a rock in the distance. She ran to it, starvation driving her forward. Only to find that it was a rattler catching the warmth of the morning's light. It would have been a most disastrous end to her trek. Not a fitting end for someone who'd endured so much.

She reluctantly accepted the fact that her only chance for survival was to be picked up by a passerby. Her legs would carry her no further. Mouse stumbled up the drainage ditch and back onto the asphalt of the roadway.

Mouse tripped over a rock, sending her to the ground. The impact kicked up dust. The dryness in her throat fought against the dirt's introduction into her open mouth. Coughing, she crawled forward slowly. Her palms seared by the hot surface. She waited. She did not fear death. She had been surrounded by it since before she could remember. Sometimes it came swiftly. Other times it was slow. But it always came. She was aware that nobody could escape its eventuality. In that simple understanding about the fragility of life, she found peace.

It was not death that she feared. It was the failure of the promise she'd made. Her father had given her the tools to endure under the harshest of circumstances and prevail against all odds. But her mother had given her the will to survive. Mouse was a balance of her father's strength and her mother's wisdom. Her mother took ill shortly after her father's disappearance. Terrified that Mouse would be left in the streets of Juarez to fend for herself, she entrusted her life savings to a man that promised to get her daughter to the United States.

Mouse sat on the side of the road and thought of her mother's dying wish and the words of their last conversation. "Mouse, my littlest angel, it's time. Time for both of us to go. The road that you must travel is much longer than mine, but I will be waiting for you at its end. Promise me that you will make a life for yourself in America. Promise me that you will find your way."

The thought of her mother's words reverberated within Mouse's mind. She welled up with the emotion of her failure as she prepared to die all alone on a highway in a country she never had a chance to know. No tears fell because her dehydrated body had long since been able to produce water. She lay down, finding a patch of dirt that was still cool enough to touch. She let in death, as the ground began to rumble.

Weightless. Floating. Just as she'd always thought it would feel. *Death is easy.* The sound of a guitar began to fill her ears. Confused by the sound she thought, *Why are the gates of Heaven playing American country music?* A flicker of white light blinded her. As her vision cleared she saw a tiny hula girl wiggling in her grass skirt. *Heaven is a confusing place.* And then the light dissipated. The sights and sounds faded into obscurity.

"How long's she been out?" The woman's voice was shrill.

"Darned if I know. Found her layin' on the side. Thought it was a dead fox when I first came up. I mean, Jeez Louise, never seen nothin' like it." The man's voice pitched high and low in an animated fashion as he spoke.

"When'd they say they'd be here?" the woman asked, pointedly.

"Dunno. I called 911 and told them I was gonna bring her here. So, I'm guessin' bout half hour?" the man replied.

"I'm gonna fix'er up a whole mess a grub. Can I getcha some too?" She asked, sweetening up her tone.

"Coffee's fine for me, hun. Much appreciated." He smiled as she walked away, taking a moment to appreciate the ample figure of the departing waitress.

Bertram Hadsworth had been coming to Ma's Diner since he was a boy. And he'd been flirting with Jackie Masternick since before he could remember. The years did nothing to increase his confidence and, at forty-two, he'd never upped the nerve to ask her out on a date. *Someday*, he told himself. Today would not be that day. Today, he needed to get this young girl help.

The diner began to fill with the regulars. None took much notice of Bertram until they saw the girl slumped in the booth seat across from him. But these were good country folk and they only gave a quick glance before going about their business. People in Bertram's town didn't mind the affairs of others. It wasn't their way.

The bell above the entrance to Ma's Diner rang out the newest arrival. Bertram had been close to right about the Sherriff's timeline. Thirty-seven minutes after Bertram had placed the call Deputy Bill Parsons entered. He stood quietly on the worn out welcome mat, stopping at the door's threshold. He surveyed the patrons. Bertram nodded discretely at the lawman, who registered the gesture and responded by walking toward him. Mouse stirred but didn't wake.

"She's sure a tiny little thing. Doesn't look too good neither. How long would you say that she's been out?" Parsons asked.

Bertram took a moment to look at the clock on the wall, performing the calculation. "Since I dun found her bout an hour ago. Don't know how long before that."

Parsons gingerly bent down as the starched creases of his light brown shirt gave way to his new position. He placed two fingers across her wrist and waited for the answer. The formed plastic of his shiny pistol belt squeaked loudly as he stood abruptly.

Parsons took another hard look at the girl and grabbed at his lapel mic. Clicking down on the plastic button, he relayed to headquarters, "217 at the Diner. I'm gonna need those medics to expedite." His voice was steady, but there was an air of urgency to his request.

"D'ya think she'll be okay?" Bertram asked of the deputy. Concern stretched across his wide sunburnt forehead as he looked intently at the unconscious child on the seat in front of him.

"I hope. Time will tell. Once I get her situated with the medics, I'm going to need to get the details from you." Parsons said, gravely.

Deputy Parsons glanced around the small diner and could see that the other customers were trying hard to mind their own business, but his presence made that difficult. Forks and spoons clinked as they feigned interest in their meals.

Chapter 7

"How long are we talking?" Harrison asked into the cellphone.

"If I knew I'd tell you, but at least a couple hours. Maybe more. No way to know for sure, until one of the other girls decides to enlighten us with some conversation," Jones relayed, standing with one foot in the room and the other on the landing. It was like he was standing in-between two completely alternate worlds.

"I make no promises. But if you're going to have any luck in picking up that scent, then it'll be with Jasper." Harrison's confidence in his partner's ability was clearly evident in his words and tone.

"I've heard. That's why I requested you by name," Jones said, allowing for the compliment to be received. "We've got a good group of K9 teams here in the city, but from what I hear you two are local legends."

"I can be on location in less than thirty. I just got to clean Jasper up from his last adventure. He's still got a little bit of meth-head stuck in his teeth." Harrison and

Jones both laughed at this. Harrison quickly returned to the business at hand and added, "If you could minimize the people in the room until I get there, then that would help me out. And don't let anyone else touch the item. The less contact, the better the scent."

"Consider it done. See ya soon." Jones hung up the call and stared off into the distance, looking at the city he called home and thinking about how much his current assignment has changed his perspective of it.

Jasper was greedily lapping up the water from his large metal bowl. His second bottle of water since the conclusion of his early morning's jaunt through the hilly terrain. Harrison was accustomed to days like this, where the request for his services seemed to stack. He also had quiet days. But this apparently was not going to be one of those. Jasper's fur around his mouth was soaked with the Evian water. For some reason, unbeknownst to Harrison, it was the only water that Jasper would drink. He often laughed at the quirkiness of his K9 partner. Harrison allowed his four-legged friend to finish before wiping the last bits of blood from his jawline.

"C'mon boy! Let's go. Time to do God's work," Harrison said, and Jasper's ears perked.

God's work. Their code. There was a truth behind those words. Harrison bore witness to the awful things that people do to one another. He'd come to the conclusion that God must be pretty busy to let these things slide by, unpunished. He felt the calling at an early age and figured that maybe he could help out in lessening the Lord's burden.

Travis County was an expansive jurisdiction that included the state's capital of Austin. Jasper's early morning track of the tweaker who'd fled after a botched home invasion took place in the outskirts of the City of Round Rock. Not too far from Austin. He told the detective thirty minutes but would probably be there before the estimated timeframe. He had to make one stop before he headed to the scene.

Harrison pulled into the parking lot of Round Rock Donuts. It was tradition. Whenever a call took him to the city, he made sure he paid the iconic bakery a visit. Rusty Harrison did not break from his regimented dietary restrictions except for on special occasions. And this was one of those. He was back out in less than two minutes. A chocolate-covered doughnut for him and a glazed for his partner. The two savored the flakey treat as they sped south on I35 toward Austin.

"I'll be right back, buddy," Harrison said, as he closed the door to his cruiser.

Jasper stared at him with his large dark eyes. The golden hair that filled in around his eyes gave a softness to his intimidating stature. The car was left running with the air on full blast. The fan built into the right-side rear passenger window blew out the interior heat and created a continuous flow of air for Jasper.

"Up here," a portly man in a sweat-soaked button-up shirt called down from the second-floor landing.

"Rusty Harrison." His hand extended to the detective after making quick work of the stairs.

"Kemper Jones. I'm glad you were available. You were atop a shortlist of preferred trackers," Jones said, extending his hand with the compliment.

"Where's the shoes?" Harrison asked.

"Inside on the floor near the head of the far side bed. I hadn't moved them and barely touched them. We thought there were only seven girls, but this extra pair of shoes has me concerned." The implication of the statement was clear.

"Understood. I'm going to bring my partner up and we'll get started. Do me a favor and grab your fittest patrolman to call the track. We move fast," Harrison said, recalling the failed support from Officer Fontaine during their earlier adventure.

Jones looked around for a minute and then called to a tall thin black officer talking with a neighboring guest. "Calhoun, you're going to run the track with Harrison."

The officer smiled and thanked Jones with his eyes. Running a track obviously trumped the door-to-door canvass for the young, fit officer.

Harrison clicked the button on his fob and the latch to the rear door of his cruiser made an audible popping sound. Jasper nudged it open and trotted up to Harrison, tapping his wet nose against his partner's hand. Rusty untethered the leash that crossed his shoulder like a bandolier. He clipped it to the collar and the two proceeded into Room 204. Harrison guided Jasper to the shoes. He couldn't help noticing how small the sneakers were. A sick feeling filled his stomach at this reality. Jasper sniffed hard and then popped his head up. His right ear flickered. The track had begun.

Jasper moved onto the landing and out to the stairs that he had just ascended minutes before. The Malinois's head swiveled while he moved looking for the scent that had been cast from the owner of those little shoes.

Jasper held the track. He moved quickly as they broke from frontage road that paralleled I35, heading west on East 12th Street. Calhoun had no trouble keeping up. He was stride for stride with the duo, calling in radio updates as they progressed. They passed through the grassy park that surrounded the State Capitol building. Jasper stopped only long enough to avoid a passing vehicle, but the streets were quiet on a Sunday morning.

Jasper stopped at the intersection with Rio Grande Street. The track had taken them on a straight line west, but it appeared that it may be lost. Jasper shifted his body.

"Do you want me to call it?" Calhoun asked, after giving this latest location over the radio. Calling the track would announce that it was over.

"Give him a minute. He'll tell me when it's done. And he hasn't yet," Harrison said, awaiting the familiar look from Jasper that the scent was gone. The dog's head continued to push around the ground, bobbing up and down slightly.

The pull of the leash caught Harrison off guard. The track had resumed, still pushing west. They doglegged south onto North Lamar Boulevard, but only for a block until they pushed west again. This time on West 11th Street. Jasper stopped at the T-intersection with Baylor Street, scanning the tiered rise of concrete ahead. The brightly-colored walls of the Hope Outdoor Gallery were set in the middle of the old Austin neighborhood. Graffiti artists shared their talent without reprisal. A unique and vibrant visual representation of Austin's massive artistic patronage.

Jasper left the street, hitting the dirt-covered path that intertwined with the kaleidoscope of images. His movements were more erratic now as he zigzagged up the slow rise. This time, when he stopped, Harrison saw his furry partner's ear twitch and matched the direction of his gaze. Then he saw it. The surrounding walls shadowed the form sprawled on the ground.

"Platz," Harrison said. The command given, Jasper took a prone position at his foot. "Blieb." With that last utterance, Jasper would not move until told to do so. Then Harrison directed his attention to Calhoun. "Lets' go."

The two men approached slowly, not wanting to scare the girl. She did not react to their approaching footsteps. Both officers crouched low and it was Calhoun that spoke first.

"Hey sweetheart, I'm Darius. We're here to help you."

His words were kind and his voice smooth. They'd be a welcome sound to anyone in distress.

Unfortunately, the small girl's ears would never hear those words. As Harrison gently rocked her shoulder, he could feel the damp stickiness of her blood-soaked shirt. Panicking, he rolled her from her side to her back to check her vitals. She was cold to the touch. Those vacant eyes would never be able to capture the beauty of her surroundings. Harrison and Calhoun exchanged pained glances. The two strong men momentarily emotionally crippled by the girl that lay before them.

Rusty bent forward, placing his hands on his knees. The dead girl brought up an image he'd long since repressed. It dizzied him. He swayed, fighting back against the memory.

Chapter 8

It was quiet except for the crunching and slurping of the small girl hunched over the tray of food. While chewing, she would lift her eyes and scan the room's interior. The walls were a dull color, like an offspring of beige and gray. No pictures. No windows. A square table and some cheap plastic chairs were its only furnishings. Mouse swallowed and returned to the mountain of food in front of her. She forked a mouthful of syrup-covered pancakes into her mouth, breathing through her nose.

"Look at her. She eats like a Coyote in Spring," Deputy Parsons watched on the monitor.

The camera affixed to the corner of the interview room relayed the live feed of the girl's ravenous consumption of the food generously provided by Jackie Masternick of Ma's Diner.

"I wonder how long it's been since she last ate?" Anaya Patel said this with genuine concern. "She could make herself sick."

"The doc said that it was hard to tell, but at least a few days without food and water. The IVs really helped. I thought she was a goner. A few more hours and she probably would've been," Parsons relayed.

"I'm going to go in and say hello."

"I don't think she speaks English," Parsons said.

"Why do you think that?" Anaya asked.

"Cuz she didn't say nothin' to me." A defensive response by the lawman.

"Maybe she didn't like you," Anaya said, lessening the blow with a smile and wink.

"I'll be watching from out here if you two need anything," Parsons said, accepting his role.

"Will do. Thanks for the call, Bill. Hopefully, we can get her some help."

The door opened slowly, and Anaya Patel's slender body stood at the threshold. She did not enter the room. Mouse looked at her but said nothing. Anaya allowed the girl time to evaluate her. Damaged children were like stray dogs. They needed time to acclimatize to new surroundings and new people. Anaya knew this better than most and she was patient. The girl's eyes shot back to the food. The initial threat assessment was apparently over.

"Can I come in?" Anaya asked the small girl. The first step to establishing trust was to empower.

No words. The girl only moved her head in the slightest of nods.

"Thank you," Anaya said, genuinely.

Nothing. A long slurp of water filled the silence.

"I know that you are hungry, but you may want to slow down. Too much food too fast could make you sick," Anaya said.

Anaya had a gentle way. It came naturally to her. Her kindness was a byproduct of her own childhood trauma.

The small girl paused, contemplating the words. The fork balanced between her thumb and forefinger. It hovered above the diner's generous portions. She put it down on the table. The subtle standoff over, she cast her eyes toward Anaya but ensured that she avoided making direct eye contact.

"I'm Anaya. I work for an agency called Child Protective Services. My job is to help children like you. And I want you to know that you're in good hands because I'm very good at what I do," Anaya said, knowing the importance of establishing primacy. She needed the girl to believe in her abilities if any early trust was to be built.

Anaya had gauged that the girl had an excellent grasp of English without ever asking. She had appropriately responded non-verbally to everything said up to this point.

"I would like to know your name so that I have something to call you by," Anaya said, softly.

Nothing.

"Is there something people call you? It doesn't have to be your real name." Anaya said, using a line she'd used many times before.

Anaya knew that this girl might fear some reprisal if her legal name was given. Kids in her position often worried about their captors finding them or getting deported. She always liked to give the nickname option as an icebreaker.

The small girl seemed to make herself even smaller as she said, "Mouse. My name is Mouse."

Anaya was correct. This girl had an excellent command of the English language.

"Mouse it is then. Thank you for that," Anaya said, satisfied that the first connection had been developed. She smiled at the little girl.

Mouse's cheeks twitched momentarily but she did not smile. In the safety of her temporary surroundings, she allowed some of the tension to release. But she remembered that she still had promises to keep.

Chapter 9

Nick pulled into the parking garage of the massive building that rose up in the heart of downtown Austin. He'd already coordinated with the booking sergeant prior to his arrival so that they could arrange to have Richard Pentlow prepared. Nick entered through the secured law-enforcement-only entrance to the facility after showing his credentials to the jailer. The bustling movement of police officers, jail personnel and inmates looked like an ant mound that had been poked with a stick. *Must have been a busy night.*

Nick walked to the main desk area and again showed his credentials. "Agent Lawrence to see inmate Pentlow. I spoke with Sergeant Willis on the phone and he said that he'd have him ready for me," Nick said.

"He's in interview room number three. I'll take you to him." The jailer was friendly but direct. The interview of Pentlow was obviously low on his priority list and it was evident that he wanted to get back to the task of preparing for the morning's arraignments.

"Busy night?" Nick asked, making small talk as the two walked into the brightly-lit corridor containing a row of closed doors along the right-hand side.

"Pretty typical fallout from a Saturday night," the guard said and shrugged as if the volume of newly-arrested people was barely a blip on his radar. "Here you go. The room has a camera system that will record your interview. We can get you a copy before you leave. One of our deputies, Dan Shelton, is inside with him and will standby outside the door while you do your thing."

"Thanks. I'm not sure how long this will take," Nick said, knowing that every interview was different, and the timeframe was dependent on so many factors.

"Well, he's set to see the judge at around ten, so you've only got about an hour," the jailer said, opening the door to the interview room.

The county did daily arraignments. A judge would hear any new arrests that came in through the night and early morning hours. The probable cause for the custody would be reviewed and a bond would be set.

"I guess I'd better get started then," Nick said, with a smile.

Nick entered the room and nodded at Shelton who exited without saying a word. As the door clicked shut, he stood for a moment acclimatized to the room and the man nervously seated a few feet away. Nick took the seat across from him. The man's head remained down. The top of which was thinned, and wisps of dirty blond hair lay over his bald spot.

"Good morning, Mr. Pentlow. I'm Agent Lawrence with the FBI," Nick said, extending his hand.

Richard Pentlow seemed shocked by the Agent's greeting. Nick knew why. Nobody liked a pedophile and his treatment had probably been less than hospitable since his arrival. Nick knew this and, by design, knew the importance of his outreached hand. Pentlow wiped his clammy palms on his pants and took the agent's hand, giving it a weak shake.

"How are you holding up? Can I get you anything?" Nick asked, in a tone that sounded genuine.

It was an act. Nick would like nothing more than to reach across the table and choke the life out of the man. He'd learned that would do more harm than good. Kindness and compassion, even when well-faked, were instrumental in developing rapport. The key ingredient to getting a confession. Nick had mastered the ability of putting aside his personal feelings in these investigations. He'd found the appropriate release for that harbored rage. It was not now and definitely not here.

"I'm fine, I guess," Pentlow said, meekly.

"Alright. Well, let's get the formalities out of the way," Nick said, as he slowly pulled a sheet of paper from his folder.

Nick went through line by line of the Miranda warning, reading it aloud as Pentlow followed along silently. Nick verified that Pentlow understood each piece through verbal confirmation and annotation in the form of his initials. Pentlow signed the bottom of the page, authorizing Nick to speak with him.

"How long have you lived in the Austin area?" Nick asked, catching Pentlow off guard.

People based their idea of what a police interview should look like from poorly developed Hollywood scripts. Television and movies rarely showed this aspect of an interrogation. They cut to the dramatic confrontation, but Nick knew that the likelihood of confession was built in these subtle moments of connection between suspect and interviewer.

"Huh? Oh, about three years," Pentlow answered.

"Where did you move from?" Nick asked. To an outsider, it would appear that Nick was genuinely interested in Richard Pentlow's life.

"Oregon. Grew up there, but then a job opportunity presented out this way," Pentlow said, meekly.

Pentlow was comfortable talking about his job. It was a safe area. Nick needed these contextual points to fall back on if the bond weakened at the later stages of the interview.

"Was your wife supportive of the move?" Nick asked, gauging Pentlow's reaction to the introduction of his spouse into the conversation.

Pentlow gave a miniscule grimace. Too early to tell if the facial tick was related to his present circumstance or a general disdain for his wife.

"I guess. Well, not really. She had no friends or family out this way. Once we got here, she's pretty much become a recluse," Pentlow said, lowering his eyes.

"That's got to be tough. How is your relationship with her?" Nick asked, taking an early risk.

He was under the time crunch and needed to extract as much information as he could before the arraignment. The chance of Pentlow talking after that would drop drastically. In Nick's experience the best opportunity to confront an arrestee was after booking, but before intermingling with the judicial process. Once bond was posted, suspects did not typically feel the need to speak with police. Their initial desperation would be dashed with the inject of a defense attorney's advice.

"Relationship?" Pentlow showed the first signs of emotion. Anger.

"Not good?" Nick prodded.

"That's an understatement. All she does is care for her kids. I'm the odd man out in the house," Pentlow said, spitting his frustration at Nick.

Nick caught something in Pentlow's statement and inquired further, "You said her kids. Are you not their biological father?"

"Her son and daughter are from two different dads. Not mine. I really do care for them though."

Pentlow said this last part for effect. He was trying to win Nick's approval. That's a good thing. It meant that subconsciously he valued Nick's opinion of him. That could be manipulated to an advantage as the conversation progressed.

"I'm sure you do. I have no question about your dedication. I mean, look at all you've done for them. You took this job out here to give them a better life. To give your wife more. Does she appreciate the sacrifices that you've made?"

Nick asked this by design. He needed Pentlow to see Nick as someone who understood his plight. He'd be more likely to talk to a supportive ear.

"No. She's treated me like shit since we moved here." Pentlow paused for a moment and then continued,

"Sorry for the language. I don't mean to sound crass, but it just upsets me."

The irony was not lost on Nick. A man in custody for raping an eleven-year-old girl had just apologized for cursing. "Treated like shit?" Nick broached.

"Well, it's kind of personal."

"I'd really like to understand you better. It's important to me. Your well-being is important to me," Nick said.

It was an absolute lie. He wanted to shove his fist down the perv's throat but that would do nothing to help the case. It would do nothing to help those girls.

"Thank you. Do you know that you're the first person to treat me like a human being since this morning?" Pentlow said, sadly.

This comment was a verbal confirmation that Nick had struck interrogator gold in the rapport phase of the interview. He could slowly apply the pressure. Slowly break the man seated across from him.

"Richard, we are under a time crunch this morning. You're going to be seeing the judge in less than an hour." Nick paused for effect and then continued, "I'm not going to sugar coat this. You're facing some very serious charges and the cards are stacked against you."

"I didn't do anything! I told the cops that I heard a girl scream and I went in to help. I didn't touch that girl!" Richard said, desperately. His eyes widened, pleading for Nick to believe him.

"If you're going to stick to that story, then I'm going to leave." Nick closed his notebook and slid the chair back slowly.

Richard Pentlow's head dipped and his body slumped. Nick observed this pathetic display of defeat as he made his way toward the door.

As Nick reached for the door handle he looked and said, "I'm you're only chance at getting you any consideration with the court. This door closes behind me and the opportunities leave with me."

"Wait!" Pentlow shot a glance at the agent.

"Would you like to talk? To really talk about what happened?" Nick asked, firmly. The feigned kindness he'd shown Pentlow was dissipating.

"Yes," Pentlow muttered, softly.

Taking his seat, Nick stared seriously at the man in front of him. He sighed, as if annoyed at this game, and began the renewed conversation, "Look there're some things that you need to understand before we begin again."

Pentlow nodded but didn't speak.

"You were caught in a room with an eleven-year-old girl tied to a bed and six others locked in the bathroom. Not sure there's any way that you can spin that to your advantage," Nick said, holding back his disdain for the man before him. He continued, "Your friends and family will abandon you. The prosecution will destroy you. And prison. Well prison will be a living hell for you."

"I can't go to prison! You've got to help me," Pentlow whimpered, rubbing his face wildly as if trying to wake from a terrible nightmare.

"I don't make the deals," Nick said, coldly.

"Then what good are you to me," Pentlow said, lashing out in frustration.

"I'm the guy that talks to the prosecution. I'm the guy that tells them you're fully cooperating with my investigation. And if you don't bullshit me then maybe, just maybe, I can arrange to have you set up in isolation so that you don't have to be in gen pop," Nick said.

"Gen pop?" Pentlow asked.

"General population. Do you know how many inmates have children? Even the nastiest of prisoners will hate you. They'll find out what you did. They always do. And when that happens it'll be a fate worse than death," Nick said, allowing Pentlow's racing mind to fill in the gap. The unsaid threat.

"Maybe I'll beat this thing. Maybe my attorney will fix it," Pentlow said, weakly.

"Good luck with that." Nick shook his head, punctuating the truth in his statement and then continued, "So, back to what I was saying. You need to come clean on this if you want any semblance of court consideration."

Richard Pentlow let out a long breath and sat silently with his arms folded. Nick waited patiently, allowing the quiet of the room to add its own pressure.

His arms unfolded and Pentlow rubbed his moist hands on his jeans. He looked up but barely made eye contact and said, almost in a whisper, "Okay. I'll tell you everything. Just please help me."

Nick wondered if that little girl had pleaded with him when tied to the bed in the motel. He swallowed hard, suppressing his overwhelming desire to hurt the man seated across from him. He didn't give way to this emotion, knowing that it would only stall his chances of finding the men responsible for selling those girls. Nick clicked his pen and waited for Pentlow to begin.

Chapter 10

Rusty Harrison slumped against the side of his Ford Crown Victoria as Jasper lapped at his Evian-filled bowl. He repetitively ran his fingers through the soft hair atop his partner's head. The dog's ears flickered with each pass. Rusty's eyes were vacant and he used this quiet moment to try and clear his mind. Seeing the lifeless girl had rocked him to his core. He could still feel her blood on his hands even after rinsing them three times. He looked down, wondering if they would ever feel clean again. He'd seen bad things before and was aware of the aftermath, knowing that feeling would stay with him for a long time to come.

"How are you holding up?" Jones asked, with a genuine compassion.

The dark humor of the police had a line not to be crossed and dead children topped that shortlist.

"I want a part in this," Harrison said, looking directly into the eyes of the investigator.

"You've done your part. And I really appreciate your help," Jones placated.

"You can use me any way you see fit. I just want to be there when we grab the guy who did this. Jasper has a hankering for assholes like him," Harrison said, through the tension in his jaw.

"I'll see what I can do. It would be nice to have a dedicated K9 asset," Jones said.

His phone chimed, and he pulled it from his pocket, pressing it to his ear as he stepped away from Harrison.

"Did he talk?" Jones asked.

"Yes. He gave me what he knew, but I think we might get more specifics when we hear back from Digital," Nick responded.

"Let me guess. Some website with a number and a cash exchange?" Jones said, knowing that the pattern for these types of deals.

"Pretty much. It sounds like the description of the handler is close to that given by the manager for the Jose Torres guy, who'd rented the room. Pentlow claimed that it was the first time he had done this. A lie, but I do think that this is the first time that he used this particular service provider." Nick said, knowing that by the time a pedophile was caught there was typically a long line of undocumented victims.

"Why do you think this was the first time he used this girl's handler?" Jones asked.

"When I explained that the girls in that motel room were probably being managed by very dangerous people, he was terrified. The fear of reprisal seemed to really shake him," Nick replied. "He told me that the Torres guy took a picture of his driver's license."

"Makes sense. These girls are definitely not locals. It looks like Pentlow's perversion might've crossed paths with an organized trafficking group," Jones said, stating the obvious.

"Yup. How long until your digital guys have something back?" Nick asked. He was prepared to offer the Bureau's services but knew that Austin had a comparable unit.

"Top priority, especially with the latest," Jones responded, realizing that he hadn't yet relayed the information about the dead girl. An oversight, understandable under the situation.

There was a morning breeze and the plastic covering over her body flapped, making a rustling sound. A sad reminder of the small child who lay lifeless underneath it on the concrete rise behind him.

"Huh?"

"There was an eighth girl. We ran a track to find her," Jones said, slowly bleeding out the information. "I called you but realized that you were probably in the jail. No cell reception." Jones knew that Nick wouldn't feel slighted but added it anyway.

"How old?"

"My guess is between nine and eleven," Jones said, quietly.

"Is she willing to talk?" Nick asked, with an air of optimism.

"Can't. She's dead," Jones said. Silence followed. The two hardened men knew that there were no offerings to be made. No ease could be given to the harsh reality of the girl's death.

"How?" Nick said. Any trace of his previous hopefulness was dashed from his tone.

"Stab wounds. Multiple." Jones drifted away, deep in thought.

"Jesus. I'm in my car and will meet you out there in a few," Nick said.

"Don't bother. Homicide is here. Their techs have already started processing the scene. It's still our case, but they want to ante in on the body," Jones said, with a discernable annoyance in his voice.

Nick had worked with Jones enough to know that having another detective unit poking around his case was cause enough to send the rotund investigator into a brisket-eating frenzy.

"Well, it's still our case, right?" Nick asked, somewhat rhetorically.

"Of course," Jones said.

"Then let's work the shit out of it and find the bastards that did this!"

Nick was rarely animated, but this case hit his hot button. He was fired up. Never good to be on Nicholas Lawrence's bad side.

Chapter 11

"What do you plan to do with her now?" Bill Parsons asked.

"She needs rest. I'm going to bring her to my office. I've got a small bedroom that comes in handy for situations like these." Anaya paused, her mind drifting back to when she had been in a similar circumstance.

She'd always wished that somebody had shown her the same kindness. It was one of the many reasons that she had chosen the path that she was on now.

She snapped out of her momentary lapse and back to the present. Anaya continued, "Mouse will probably have more to say once she recoups a bit. Sleep is a magical thing, when it comes to recovery."

"Mouse?" Parsons asked, raising an eyebrow at social workers comment.

"Yup. Mouse. That's what she told me to call her. I like it. And I like her," Anaya said, softly.

"Don't go getting too attached, you hear? You know that as soon as ICE gets involved they're going to send her back," Parsons said. There was an odd combination of sincerity and cynicism in his comment.

Anaya could not tell from Parsons inject where he fell on the immigration debate. Nor did she care. Politics were for the politicians. Her concern was for people. And right now, the only person that mattered to her was Mouse.

Mouse slept for the entire drive to the Child Protective Services headquarters building. Groggy, Mouse followed the social worker like a child being marched off to bed. Anaya's office space was quaint. She spent most of her time out of it, doing fieldwork. She'd always felt that she could do more good being out with the people she was trying to help rather than hiding behind her computer, as many of her coworkers did. She'd realized that this was why she was an island of isolation. It had always been that way for her. Both professionally and personally. She hoped the latter eventually changed but so much of her was invested in the children she worked with that little time was left for anything else. *An unbalanced life*, her last attempt at a boyfriend had taunted.

"I know that it's not much, but it's pretty comfy. Trust me. I know," Anaya said to Mouse, as she opened the door adjacent to her desk.

"Thank you," Mouse said. She entered and plopped onto the cot. It barely creaked under the minimal weight of her tiny frame.

Mouse rolled away from the open door. Away from Anaya. And curled into a ball, making herself seem even smaller. Anaya lay a soft blanket over her and retreated, pulling the door shut.

Mouse lay still. Her eyes flickered but sleep would not come. The darkness of the room lifted as her vision adjusted. No furnishings but the bed and a few paintings. It was better accommodations than she'd had in a long time. *Too bad I won't be staying long.*

"She's sleeping. She is going to need time. I don't know. Maybe she will never talk about it. Just give me a little bit before you make any calls. It's not like she's a fugitive on the run for murder. She's a kid." Anaya spoke quietly but the thin walls did little to mask the words.

It was obvious to Mouse that the nice woman must be speaking on the phone because no other voice could be heard. *Who was she talking to? Probably the cop.* And Anaya was wrong about one thing... *I am a killer.*

The door to the office closed and Mouse could hear the clack of the kindhearted Anaya Patel's shoes as she walked away. She knew that she would not see her again and, for some reason, the thought made Mouse sad.

She sat up and gathered the extra clothes that Anaya had laid out for her. She put them into the black backpack that was also gifted to her and slid the straps over her slight shoulders. She crept out into the office, leaving behind the first bed she'd slept on in weeks. The office door was unlocked. Now opened, she scanned the surrounding cubicles. The few people around did not seem to notice or care. They were busy going about their routine.

Mouse moved quickly but smiled as she passed the other workers. They must have been accustomed to small children walking around the office area because they smiled back and continued about their business. She heard Anaya's voice coming from a break room. The smell of burnt coffee filled the air as Mouse shot past the open space and headed directly for the elevator. No halting command shouted from Anaya. She'd navigated without detection. It would hopefully be a while before Anaya would realize that Mouse was gone. She'd heard her tell the person on the phone that she needed rest. That would give Mouse an opportunity to get some distance between her and the police.

The small girl stood outside the white concrete exterior of the Child Protective Services building and allowed her eyes to adjust to the bright afternoon sunlight. Mouse didn't want to be found and sent back. Or worse, found and killed.

She had her mother's promise to keep.

Chapter 12

Nick saw Jones pacing in front, pulling hard from the cigarette in his lips. He parked the Jetta and walked to him.

"Those things will kill you," Nick called out, half-joking.

"Gotta die of something. At least I'll enjoy myself until the end," Jones chuckled.

Nick didn't really judge the man. He'd smoked overseas. It had been in contradiction to his fitness regime, but in war the rules didn't apply. It was a way of passing time. He'd grown up listening to his father's story, told repeatedly, about his youthful days as a chain smoker. His dad would then finish his retelling in dramatic fashion, stating that on one particular day the surgeon general announced that smoking cigarettes could cause cancer. He told Nick that he quit that day. Never took another drag. His father's strong will had been instilled in him. Nick had heard his father retell that story too many times to count. As young man he used to roll his eyes, but now that his father was gone he'd give anything to hear it one more time. Nostalgia gave way to reality and he walked with Jones to the building's front doors.

The doors opened and the two were overwhelmed with the familiar scent. Four employees were busy with a mop. The tendrils of which were soaked a dark red. A sloshing sound could be heard as it brushed over the surface.

"Now, this is where we will break this case wide open," Jones said, slapping Nick on the shoulder.

The familiar tingle trickled down to Nick's fingers.

Nick smiled wide and said, "I like the way you think. But if I worked every case with you I'd probably be medically retired."

"Let's do this," Jones said, moving into the threshold of The Salt Lick and passed the round stone-encased grill.

A pitmaster's mop slapped against a large rack of ribs, sizzling as the hot embers took on the excess.

The two sat on a bench in the seat-yourself-style restaurant. Nick got the pulled pork and Jones ordered enough brisket and burnt ends to feed three people. This case had obviously pushed Jones's BBQ intake to an all-time high, especially with it turning into a homicide.

"Where are we at with this thing?" Nick said, bringing the focus back.

"Like I said on the phone, Homicide is going to work the body. Better for us so we can stay on the move. The detective in charge of that side of it is Roger Williams. He's good. No ego. He'll keep us in the loop throughout. No pissing contest and backstabbing with him," Jones relayed.

"That's good news," Nick said, thankful at the prospect that office politics would not interrupt the flow of their investigation. He added, "Alright, so they've got the body. Based on what you saw, how much do you think they're going to be able to get from it?" Nick asked.

He knew that every scene told a tale but, unlike the movies, it was sometimes an elusive one.

"Not sure. Time will tell, but if I was a betting man then I'd guess that there won't be much in the way of usable evidence," Jones said. "Especially if we're dealing with pros."

"Maybe we'll get lucky and some morning jogger or reluctant witness will call in with a description of the doer. I doubt it. But wishful thinking," Nick replied.

"Our best bet is going to come from one of the girls. They're at headquarters now and CPS has already started the process. I'm going to check in with them after we get something in our stomachs," Jones said.

The large detective salivated at the mention of his upcoming meal and rubbed his tummy for added effect.

"I've got one stop to make and then I'll meet you over there," Nick said, the frustration of that stop evident in his voice.

Jones seemed to have registered this but refrained from inquiry, further distracted by the plate of food that slid into his view. Foregoing the fork, Jones grabbed burnt end and dropped it into his mouth. The two ate in silence, replenishing their bodies for the arduous task ahead.

Nick had done his research before making his move back to Texas. Pine Woods retirement community seemed like a perfect balance of comfort and medical assistance. His mother made the move with a dignified grace, as she'd done with all of life's hurdles. It hurt Nick to have her leave the home where she'd spent the majority of her adult life. The place she'd raised her family. Memories of those times were fading rapidly.

The hardship that his mother endured with his brother's suicide had been unbearable. No parent should ever have to bury their child, but she did. And she somehow managed to shoulder its weight. The loss of Nick's dad seemed to tip the scales. He'd always felt that the dementia was her brain's way of sheltering her mind from the terrible sadness.

Nick's overwhelming sense of failure was crushing. The reality was that he couldn't give her proper care anymore as her mental health deteriorated. He uprooted her and hauled her out here, forcing her to leave behind any reminders of her past. Nick couldn't help but feel wholly responsible for her current decline in behavior. Constantly he questioned himself as to whether they should have stayed in Connecticut. *At least I'd have Izzy.*

"Is Doctor Whitmore available?" Nick asked of the receptionist positioned at the arced information desk.

"Let me check." She thumbed through a chart on her desk and continued, "Yes. Give me a second and I'll have him paged for you. Can I have your name so that I can let him know who's waiting?"

"Nicholas Lawrence. He's expecting me," Nick said, politely.

"You can wait over there, and he should be with you shortly," the woman said, with a gentle smile.

"Thank you," Nick replied.

He turned and eyed the lobby's waiting area. It was a typical arrangement of assorted couches and chairs scattered around a small wooden coffee table. Nick drifted past the pile of magazines that covered its surface and proceeded to Keurig set against the far wall. Even in the heat of the day, Nick never shied away from a cup. He never understood the iced-coffee craze. It was meant to be hot and that's the only way he drank it.

"Mr. Lawrence," Doctor Whitmore said, as he entered the lobby from the secured medical door.

"That was quick. Thanks for seeing me Doc," Nick said, turning to greet the doctor.

Nick extended his hand as the machine behind him hissed out the steaming black liquid.

"I'm glad that you made it. I know that your schedule is demanding and unpredictable," Whitmore said.

"Today is already starting to be one of those days. I figured that I should stop by during a lull because I may not be able to get back here for a few days," Nick said. His mind drifted to the image of Room 204 and then to the thought of the dead girl.

"I understand. Well then, let's not waste time," Whitmore said, gesturing with his arm toward the white double doors that read, medical personnel only.

The two walked slowly through the hallway containing the advanced-stage dementia patients. Some were seated in chairs outside their doors, vacant expressions pasted to their aging faces. No signs that they registered the world around them as the duo passed. The doctor stopped outside of a room containing one bed. Inside, Nick could make out the shape of a woman. She lay to the side, facing away from the door. She looked so frail. So small. Nick's heart sank.

"She's fine. After her outburst earlier, she has been resting. It took a lot out of her. Not so much from the physical exertion. More as a result of the mental energy expended in her moment of anger," Whitmore said, in a calm reassuring manner.

"So, this is where you want to keep her?" Nick asked. A tinge of Nick's own anger began to build inside him, but it was directed more at himself and not the doctor.

"I think that it would be best. On her good days we will bring her over to the other side to interact with the other residents," Whitmore said.

"And on the bad ones?" Nick asked.

"She would be isolated from other patients." Whitmore spoke matter-of-factly.

"This is not how I saw things going. I can't help but feel responsible for this. For the current status of things." Nick said this last part more to himself. He wasn't looking to be consoled by the doctor.

"It was an eventuality no matter where your mother was placed. Even if she had remained in her home in Connecticut, this day would have come. No point in blaming yourself," Whitmore said, with sincerity.

"Thank you." Nick saw no point in arguing his guilt with the doctor. He then turned and asked, "Is she responsive at all right now?"

"The nurse was in with her a few minutes before your arrival and said that she smiled but did not speak. I'll give you some time with her. Come find me in my office when you're done. It was the first door we passed when we entered the wing," Whitmore said, as he turned and exited the room.

Nick was left alone in the quiet. The only sound was the click of the wall clock, notifying him of each passing second. Each step toward his mother seemed like a marathon's distance. His heart pounded, and his face flushed with the impending anxiety.

"Hey, mom. How're you feeling?" Nick asked, softly. Not sure if she was awake.

His mother's eyes fluttered, "Patrick? Where have you been?" she said, with a look of bewilderment.

Nick deflated. His brother, long-since dead, is still the first face she sees. Nick had no words. He couldn't play the role today. His body went slack, and he slumped in the seat next to the bed. His hand found hers, more bony and cold than he'd remembered. He caressed the delicate hand of the woman that had raised him as his tears fell freely.

Chapter 13

The sky had opened up suddenly. A heavy downpour of rain drenched her as she ran for the shelter provided by the overpass. The cold drops gave temporary relief from the afternoon sun but had stopped almost as soon as it began. The steam that rose up from the hot concrete of the sidewalk filled the air with a humid stickiness. Her wet clothes clung tightly to her.

Mouse had left the safety of Anaya Patel's office bed a couple hours ago and had begun the task of navigating Austin's landscape. Without any knowledge of where she was going or, more importantly, where she needed to go. She'd grabbed a map from the first gas station she'd passed as she traveled down Riverside Boulevard. The money she had taken from the two men from the box truck was sufficient to get her started but wouldn't last long. Four hundred and eighty dollars would only go so far.

She wished that she could have stayed with Anaya. They would send her back. She knew it. Many people from her city had made the trip, crossing over to America. And many of them had been sent back. Mouse learned that, to survive, she must elude government officials. Even kind-hearted ones. She also knew that her return to Juarez would mean certain death. The people that arranged her travel would learn of her escape. Juarez was no longer home. So, she kept moving through the unfamiliar streets of Austin in search of her new beginnings.

"Do you think that it's connected?" Anaya asked into the cellphones receiver.

Her supervisor called while she was out driving the area looking for Mouse. Running away from a CPS office was not unheard of but running away from Anaya Patel was.

"I don't know. Let me know when you get there and if you're going to need some extra bodies to assist," her supervisor said.

"Okay. But isn't there someone else that could go? I've got to find this girl," Anaya pleaded.

"She'll turn up. I need you to take the lead on this other situation. Those kids are going to need you." Anaya's boss spoke with a gentle firmness, knowing that the words would resonate with her subordinate. She'd used the same line on her several times before.

"I'm on my way," Anaya said, with a sigh.

She was torn but vowed to return to her search for Mouse as soon as the opportunity presented. But she was also a realist and knew deep down that, as time passed, the likelihood of finding that tough little girl would diminish. She drove to Austin Police Department's headquarters.

"Anything?" Jones asked.

"Nothing. They've been sleeping for most of the time since they returned from the hospital. We've tried Spanish and English. Got nothing more than a couple glances in response," said Gary Redding, Sergeant in charge of the Special Investigations Unit.

Jones's boss gave his people the freedom and support to work a case. But, more importantly, he stepped up for his guys. Redding had already battled with Homicide to ensure that the primary case stayed with Jones and Lawrence. He now had to keep Vice from getting involved. Vice typically handled the organized sex rings, but Redding wanted this one to stay with his unit. He got approval after much debate, with the caveat that Vice would become involved when things moved from investigative to operational. Meaning Vice wanted credit for the takedown when the time came.

"Anything from medical?" Jones asked.

"They completed rape kits and they're being submitted to the lab as we speak. But that will most likely yield some potential Johns. And that's only if the DNA is already in CODIS," Redding responded, knowing that Jones was aware of this probability but saying it anyway out of routine.

"Who knows, maybe we can find another perv or two to interrogate," Jones said, wishfully.

"True. Jones, you're a true believer," Redding said with a laugh and then continued, "There was one thing that turned up during the girls' physical exams that was unique about this group. They were branded. All of them. Same brand markings."

"Branded?" Jones asked, knowing that some low-level pimps used tattoos on their girls as a way of claiming their property. It was uncommon in the international rings because they wanted to maintain a low profile. The girls were disposable. Used and thrown away.

"Yes. It's on each of their hip lines. Looks like a snake or something. Hard to tell," Redding explained.

"So, a tattoo?" Jones asked, seeking clarification.

"No. Branded." Redding held up a photo for Jones to see.

The raised skin was evident of the burn. These girls were truly branded. Like cattle. The one in the photograph must have occurred recently because of the puffiness and pink coloring. A strange mix of anger and optimism filled the seasoned investigator. Jones looked up from the picture, walked directly to his cubicle and started rifling through the files scattered about. Jones had paraphrased Einstein when anyone commented on the disorder of his desk, stating that "a messy desk is a sign of genius."

Chapter 14

Nick entered into the air-conditioned lobby of APD's headquarters, flashed his credentials to the officer behind the bulletproof glass and signed in. He moved through the metal detector, setting off the buzzer and continuing to the elevators. He waited patiently as the elevator had already been called by the woman standing in front of him. The two entered as the doors parted. She had already pressed the button for floor number five.

"Same?" she asked, ensuring that Nick didn't need to go to another floor.

"Yup," Nick responded. The woman was attractive. Her long dark hair and light brown complexion reminded him of Izzy. Or maybe it was the smell of coconut that was quickly filling the small space of the elevator's interior. Either way, he let his mind drift back to that night in the hotel room. *I'll call her as soon as I get a chance,* he told himself. His mind still reeling from the emotional release at Pine Woods. The ding of the elevator, announcing the arrival at the fifth floor, snapped him out of his momentary trance. The two exited and moved toward the sea of cubicles that made up Austin's Special Investigations Unit, or SIU.

"I swear I'm not stalking you," Nick said, with a chuckle.

"Never crossed my mind," Anaya said, shooting a playful wink back at him over her slender shoulder, exposed by her sleeveless shirt.

Jones stood as he heard Nick approaching.

"Hi, Anaya. I'm glad that you're on this with us. I see that you have met Nick?" Jones said and gestured to the man standing behind her.

"Not formally. He's just been following me around for the last five minutes or so," Anaya jested.

"Anaya Patel of Child Protective Services meet Nicholas Lawrence of the FBI," Jones announced.

The agent's hand extended, "Just Nick."

"Okay, Just Nick. It's nice to meet you," Anaya said.

She was not normally a flirtatious person and was caught off-guard by her banter.

Nick noticed that Jones appeared to be sucking in his gut. A failed effort, but one he'd never seen him make before. Maybe there is a history between the two. Or maybe just wishful thinking by Jones.

"Where are we on this?" Anaya asked, switching the conversation back to the task at hand.

"The kits are done. The girls are sleeping. Digital has the John's cell and Nick got some out of him during booking. Other than that, we're flying blind. Well, except for this," Jones said, holding up the photograph of the girl's hip.

"Is that what I think it is?" Nick asked.

He noticed a barely perceptible shutter by Anaya as Jones presented the image.

"Yup. Sure is. Branded." Jones gave the two a moment to process.

"My girl that just disappeared had the same thing. Medical said that the burn was recent. Maybe done within the last two weeks." Anaya said. A wave of panic washed over her, and she continued, "What is it? A snake?" Anaya asked.

"Maybe. Maybe a seven. Maybe just some symbol. I've been pawin' through my files," Jones said. His drawl returned.

"Anything?" Nick asked.

"Not yet."

"I'll send it to our guy and have him run it through the database," Nick said, knowing that the FBI's image recognition software had an expansive collection of pictures for comparison and could yield a potential link.

"Sounds good. I know I've seen it before. I just have to find the case file," Jones said.

"Good luck. Be careful. That pile could bury you alive," Nick said. The joke never got old. "And I know, I know, it's a sign of genius."

"I'm going to see if any of the girls want to talk. And then I'm going back out to look for my girl. She may be in a lot more danger than I originally thought," Anaya said, walking away from the two investigators.

"If anyone can get them to talk, then it will be her," Jones said, with unabashed adoration.

Whether it was professional or personal, Nick had yet to determine.

Chapter 15

"It's time. Are you ready?" His voice was steady but tense. The adrenalin was hard to contain and spread rapidly throughout the man's body.

"Born ready." A laugh accompanied the cheesy line.

"On three. Call it."

"Three... two... hit it," the commander's voice projected by the bone microphone and reverberated through the team's headsets.

The bang was loud from the street but would sound even louder to the men inside. The charges rigged to the glass shattered the facade. Two members of the unit swung long steel bars with hooked ends and raked out the remnants. Three flashbang grenades sailed through the air and into the now open storefront. They clanged across the cheap linoleum floor and slid to a stop against the wall of the ordering counter. The concussive explosion was deafening and sent a brilliant burst of light designed to overwhelm a target's senses. A critical diversion when facing dangerous men.

Stacked along the rear alleyway of the building's backside, the Hostage Rescue Team entry team listened as the noise from the flashbang filled the quiet. The initiation signal given, the team began moving toward the rear door. No words said. They'd rehearsed this operation in the weeks prior and could carry it out in their sleep.

The quick blasts from the breaching shotgun obliterated the hinges as the ram caved in the door. The team instantaneously filled the void created from where the door once stood. Another flashbang rolled ahead of the group and down into the dimly lit and narrow hallway. The entry team briefly turned their back away from the impending blast, shielding their eyes. The operators waited for the sound. The bang shook the walls, knocking off picture frames and rattling pans in the kitchen area.

Speed, surprise, and violence of action. These men knew the value of the mantra. They closed on the only door in the hallway. The point man held up one finger. No words spoken as the thick body of the breacher ambled past the line of men in cumbersome body armor. The narrow space did not allow for him to manipulate the ram effectively. Realizing that in the mockups the hallway had been wider, but now under the tight constraints the entry tool was useless. He improvised, leveling his massive shoulder into the doorframe at the nod of the team leader. The impact separated the cheaply-made door from its frame.

The breacher rolled back and out of the way as the door fell flat into the expanse of the room's small smoke-filled interior. Another flashbang immediately followed.

The five members of the entry team poured in with weapons at the ready. A small round table overturned as the three men inside scrambled. Between the cigarette smoke and that produced by the flashbang, visibility was minimal. A fat man was frantically moving across the floor on his hands and knees, cursing. It was a matter of seconds before the team had completely overwhelmed the room's three occupants.

The fat man whimpered as a size-thirteen boot stepped down on his back and pressed his wide frame to the floor. Thick zip ties were put to work, securing their hands. Satisfied, the operators righted the arrestees, using their knees to stabilize them into a seated position.

"Three in custody. All clear," the entry team leader said. His voice was as calm as if he were ordering a coffee in a drive-thru.

One of the operators stepped out of the room and into the alleyway behind J's Pizza. He pulled out his phone and pressed it to his ear, which was covered by his dry-fit balaclava. "You won't believe where I'm standing."

"Deck! Jesus your timing is impeccable. I was actually just about to call you," Nick said.

He was excited to speak to his friend. It had been several months since the two had talked. Too long. Especially after the bond they'd forged.

"J's Pizza," Declan Enright said.

"J's Pizza? What are you talking about?" Nick asked, completely baffled by the reference.

"We got three more assholes. The Translator's phone led us here. It took a while. You know how the Bureau is. Lots of surveillance before they let us make the hit. But slowly we're picking apart the organization," Declan said.

His calm voice couldn't suppress all of the excitement in grabbing three members of the elusive group known only as The Seven. A terrorist organization that terrorized the country less than a year before.

"That's awesome stuff! I wish I was there to celebrate," Nick said.

"Me too, brother. Me too. But I bet you'd rather celebrate with someone else," Declan chided. He knew that the not-so-subtle reference to Izzy would not be lost on his friend.

"Seen her lately?" Nick asked, somewhat sheepishly.

"A few weeks back at an intel briefing. But aside from that, not much. We need to get the band back together one of these days."

Declan didn't allow himself to get too close to people, but he'd lowered his guard with Nick and Izzy. Past circumstances dictated that, and now he missed the connection of that kinship.

"I'd like that. Got any vacation time coming up?" Nick asked.

"What's up, Nick? If you need me, all you have to do is ask. You know that," Declan said, with no hint of his usual sarcasm.

"I'm working a bad one here. I'll let you know. Not sure how this thing is going to play out, but I'll keep you posted. Sorry to be so vague. I'm at the early stages and don't know enough to be specific," Nick said, realizing that he wasn't sure what he was up against. He wavered and redirected the conversation, "Stay safe. Be in touch."

"You say the word and I'm there. Whatever you need. Whenever you need it," Declan said. Before hanging up, he followed with, "Give her a call, Nick."

The phone call ended, and Nick scrolled through his contacts, finding the name. Izzy's number stared back, taunting him. Nick sighed and put the phone away. He entered the black Jetta. Jones looked uncomfortable in the passenger seat of the German-designed compact sedan.

"Windows down and air on?" Jones questioned, raising an eyebrow in bewilderment.

"It's all about acclimating to the environment," Nick said, with a cocked smile.

"It feels more like you're trying to kill me. AC is my friend," Jones said, grabbing at the belly that was spilling over his belt.

The two laughed and drove off, heading toward CPS headquarters.

"I assume that someone from your office will call if any of our girls from the motel wake up and are willing to talk. Many hands make light work. Anaya could use our help finding this missing girl. Who knows, maybe she will be the piece that helps us open this thing up?" Nick said over the wind blowing through the car, as he sped away from APD's headquarters building.

Chapter 16

"I told you that I would bring you in on this if I could," Jones said, cracking a slight smile.

"I really appreciate the opportunity. I owe you," Harrison said, as he whacked his sweat-encrusted baseball cap against his thigh.

"I hope this one has a better ending."

Jones's reference to the dead girl at Hope Park was received. Rusty's eyes tightened at the mention of it. An intensity and focus seemed to take hold. Jones liked the K9 handler.

"I've just got to ask. Why are you so hell-bent on helping out with this case?" Jones asked.

Rusty sighed and busied himself in the trunk of his cruiser gathering his gear for the upcoming track, trying hard to avoid the question. Seeing that Jones was still waiting for the answer, Rusty gave in.

"My sister," Rusty said, barely audible over the idling engine of his Crown Victoria.

"Sister?" Jones asked, intrigued.

"Melanie," Rusty said, closing the trunk and looking at the detective.

Jones stood awestruck. His eyes widened, and his mouth went slack.

"Holy shit! Melanie Harrison. I never put it together. My God you're *her* brother?" Jones asked, fumbling with his words.

Rusty nodded but said nothing.

"Well that makes sense," Jones said, nodding to himself. He added, "That must've been a terrible thing for you and your family. You've done a hell of a job honoring her memory."

"Thanks. I do the best I can," Rusty offered.

He broke eye contact and freed the leash that was strapped over his shoulder.

"I best get started. Time wasted is time lost," Harrison said, freeing Jasper from the confines of the Crown Vic's backseat.

"Best of luck," Nick said, injecting himself awkwardly into the conversation.

The dog clamored out of the car and took his position next to his partner. He looked up expectantly, waiting for his handler's command. The two walked in step through the parking lot toward the main entrance of the Child Protective Service's headquarters building.

"So, what was all that about?" Nick asked.

"The thing with his sister?" Jones asked.

"Yes."

"It was a big story around here about fourteen years ago. All over the news. There was even one of those made-for-television-movies about it. Melanie Harrison went missing. Big search party. Days went by and nothing.

Then on the third or fourth day she was found. Raped and murdered. Only twelve years old at the time," Jones said.

"Jesus," Nick said, processing the horribleness of the story. "I guess that makes sense that he'd become a cop."

"Yup, but that's not the worst of it. Do you know who found her?" Jones asked, solemnly.

"My God!" Nick gasped.

"Yup. Never stopped looking for his sister. He supposedly stayed out looking for days. Slept in the woods and everything."

"I guess he's a born tracker," Nick said.

"Crazy thing. He was only ten at the time. Can you imagine what that does to a child?"

"No. No I can't," Nick said.

The two entered the Jetta and sat in silence.

Anaya had already shown Rusty the location of her office and the small room containing the cot. Her boss and coworkers were all aware that the Malinois would be in the building.

As Jasper entered the CPS office space, several gasps were expelled from the onlookers. Some gave the quiet awes of a dog lover. While others were panicked by the presence of Rusty's four-legged companion. It was always the same no matter where they went. Jasper was smaller than a German Shepherd but his coloring and snout were comparable. Rusty liked the temperament of the breed. They were intense when the need dictated but calmer than their larger counterparts. Working dogs were also a mirror of their handlers.

Jasper entered Anaya's office and Rusty guided him to the small bed. The sheets were crumpled at the foot of it. Anaya had already advised him that she hadn't touched anything since the child had run off. Jasper navigated the cramped space nudging the bedding as he circled. He inhaled loudly as he gathered the scent.

"C'mon boy. Let's find her," Harrison said to his partner.

His voice animated. The excitement contagious. Jasper perked his head up, looking at Rusty. He had the scent. Time to move.

Jasper moved quickly. His toenails clicked as he traversed the lobby of the CPS headquarters. The two burst from the sliding doors of the building's exit and into the blinding light of day. The Jetta idled quietly on the street. Jones had pleaded with Nick that they follow in the car rather than on foot. He'd agreed to the overweight detective's request, albeit reluctantly. Nick intentionally lagged behind the pair so as to minimize the interference of the car's exhaust with the scent.

The track went north on Guadalupe Street. Rusty shot a thumbs-up at the Jetta without looking back. The K9 and handler were in sync, moving quickly along the sidewalk. The dog stopped at the intersection with West 51st Street. He started to turn left but then stopped again before redirecting across the street. The two continued west. The Jetta crept slowly behind with the windows down and the air conditioning on.

Jasper walked to the intersection of Guadalupe and Lamar Boulevard and then turned around.

"Looks like he's lost the scent," Nick said.

Rusty did not look back at the two investigators. He focused on his partner.

"What is it, boy? Where'd she go?" Rusty said, in a hushed tone.

Jasper's head moved from side to side. His nose grazed the concrete of the sidewalk and then he perked up again, pulling Harrison to the double doors of the 7-11.

"I guess the dog wants a Slurpee," Jones jested.

"This might be good for us," Nick replied.

The K9 emerged a few seconds later with Rusty Harrison close behind. Jasper's snout was all over the place, dipping low, looking up, and scanning left and right. He then pulled his handler back to the storefront. Harrison gave a command and the dog sat. He looked over at the two investigators and shook his head. The track was over.

Nick and Jones exited the Jetta and approached Harrison, who was praising his dog in a high-pitched excited tone. Jasper's dark tongue lapped at his partner's face.

"Sorry guys. This is as far as it goes," Harrison said, with a trace of defeat.

"What are'ya thinkin'?" Jones asked. His accent was thicker than usual.

"Not sure. It could be that too much time has passed. Or it could be that she got into a car," Harrison responded.

"That could be a bad thing," Nick said.

"Very bad," Jones confirmed and then continued, "Rusty, thank you again for your assistance. I took into consideration your request and made a couple calls. You're going to be assigned to us as our dedicated K9 asset until we get a handle on this thing. Get some rest but keep your cell handy in case something comes up."

"That's great news! Thank you," Rusty said, rubbing the chin of his four-legged partner. "I live local, so I can be anywhere you need fairly quickly."

Nick and Jones entered the cold air of the 7-11. The contrast to the day's heat was shocking and took a moment for them to adjust.

"Oh, thank the lord!" Jones pronounced, raising his hands above his head like an invigorated worshipper.

He bypassed the clerk and walked straight to the refrigerated drink section. Jones opened the door. The suction released, and a fog of colder air rolled out. He leaned into the cooler as far as his expansive waist would allow. After what seemed like several minutes, Jones separated himself and returned to Nick at the counter with a Diet Coke.

"Welcome back," Nick joked.

"At least this guy keeps his doors shut when he runs the AC," Jones said, sarcastically.

"I've told him what we were looking for and he's got a working camera system," Nick said.

Jones rummaged his front pocket, pulling out the money to pay the clerk for the beverage.

"Anything?" Jones asked, dropping the loose change received from the purchase into the cheaply-made donation tub on the counter.

"I remember her. Not too busy on a Sunday morning. She didn't say much. Just bought a couple things and left," the clerk replied.

"You said she didn't say much. Did she say anything?" Nick said, catching the subtle hint that the clerk may have had a conversation with the girl.

"I asked her if she had money to pay for the items. We get a lot of kids that come in and try to steal. She had a backpack on, so I kept a close eye. She pulled some cash out of her pack and said something like 'I have money'," the clerk said, recalling the details.

"English?" Nick asked.

Jones was chugging down the cold soft drink but was intently listening.

"Yes," the clerk responded.

He was Indian but with very little trace of his native accent. Possibly second generation.

"Did she say anything else?" Jones said, placing the empty bottle in the recycle bin.

"She seemed nervous. Looking around a lot. When she was at the counter, I asked her if everything was alright. She nodded and told me that her mother was waiting for her in the car. Then she left," the clerk explained.

"Did you see anyone outside waiting? A car maybe?" Nick asked.

The clerk shook his head and frowned.

"Maybe the camera on the outside of the store picked something up?" Jones asked, optimistically.

"Not possible. It's a fake. Well, not a fake. It just doesn't work. Some animal chewed the wiring up a while back and I never got it fixed. More of a deterrent than anything else." The clerk's head dipped as he said this, embarrassed by the admission.

"But the internal one works, right?" Jones asked.

"Yes. Come with me to the back office and I can pull it up. It's a pretty good system," the clerk said, thumbing to the Lotto display behind him.

It took a second for Nick to see the small camera set among the rolls of colorful scratch tickets. An excellent angle to capture the face of any patron or robber.

It took only a few minutes before Nick and Jones were looking at the still frame image of the small girl. The clerk was right. The quality of the system was excellent and in color. A rarity in most investigations.

The girl did look scared. *And why wouldn't she?* People were looking for her. Not just police and social workers.

Nick snapped a photo using his cell-phone as Jones handed the clerk his business card, requesting that he forward a digital copy of the footage to his email. The two walked out into the brightness of the day.

"We've got to find this girl before someone else does," Jones said.

Nick nodded. The good thing was that she was alive as of an hour ago. Nick knew that she was on borrowed time, especially if the same guys that found the girl in Hope Park located her.

Chapter 17

She had entered the car against her will. It had pulled up as she left the 7-11 and she knew immediately that resistance would be futile. The man in the driver seat had a pleasant demeanor when he rolled down the window, but she knew that it was an act. He was a man of violence. The scars that crested his thick knuckles told the tale. Mouse had got in the car, not because of the gun, but because of the tone in his voice. He was quiet when he spoke. The heavily-tinted windows had blocked the view of any passerby to the pistol that'd been pointed at her. She recalled how he cantered it slightly with the muzzle aimed directly at her chest, using the armrest to balance it. She'd known, without a doubt, that this man would shoot her dead right outside the store. She'd seen the finality in his eyes. His only words, "Get in." Everything else implied.

"Where are you taking me?" Mouse had asked, when she'd first entered the backseat. She assumed that the man would not tell, but figured it was worth a shot.

His dark eyes glanced at her in the rear-view mirror. He said nothing, then dismissed the diminutive figure behind him, returning his gaze to the roadway in front. The driver pulled out, merging from the frontage road and onto the interstate. Mouse could feel the engine rumble with the acceleration.

With the dark-eyed man's focus on the traffic, Mouse curled into a fetal position on the bench seat. She pulled the backpack from her shoulders and wrapped her arms tightly around it. The driver took notice of her movements but did not show concern, rolling his eyes slightly. His attention was almost immediately redirected when an eighteen-wheeler crossed into his lane without signaling. The man cursed under his breath in Spanish.

The engine roared loudly as the car accelerated again. This time the effort was most likely out of anger toward the operator of the truck. A little road rage surfaced in the calm demeanor of the driver seated in front of her. Anger always gave way to opportunity. Her father taught her that. Lessons that initially were lost on her, but time and experience had proven their worth.

This drive's destination would leave her dead. Or worse. Mouse had used the backpack to conceal her right hand's movements. She had loosened the old man's belt buckle from around her slight waistline. Securing the buckle in her hand, she retracted her left hand into the concealed space shrouded by the pack and wrapped the loose end. She closed her eyes and took several controlled breaths, waiting for the *opportunity*.

The vehicle changed lanes again this time closest to the white concrete of the Jersey barriers that divided the expanse of the I35 corridor's north and southbound lanes.

The surge of the car told her that they were moving fast but she had no idea of the actual speed. Mouse knew that her next move might be her last but at least she'd be the one in control. Either way, it would be a win. *Now or never.*

Mouse launched up and, in one move, she threw the belt over the driver's head. As soon as the leather looped crested his forehead, she yanked back with all of her might, hoping to choke this man in the same manner as she had done earlier to the fat man. Her small legs jammed into the back of the driver's seat. Mouse arched back, straining the tendons of her locked arms. The car jerked violently to the right.

Her belt had not reached the driver's throat, as she'd planned. Instead, she caught him across his eyes. The effect was equally catastrophic, rendering him blind while pulling his head to the side. The driver's hands naturally followed the head's movement and he turned the steering wheel hard to the right.

The sudden movement of the car threw Mouse in the opposite direction and into the door on the left side. The belt came loose and Mouse slid to the rear floorboards. Fearing the driver's retaliation, she wedged herself down between the seats in an attempt to become as small a target as possible.

Without warning, the car veered to the left. The driver must have overcorrected. A deafening bang shook the car. Glass showered down on Mouse as she pressed her body tight against the seats.

Then silence. Nothing. No rumble of the road. No screeching tires. It was like she was floating.

The tranquility of this seemingly timeless moment was shattered by the twisting and grinding of metal and fiberglass. Mouse's gut wrenched as the car rolled. She held tight, pressing herself into the formed floor liner. The turbulence ended as abruptly as it began. Mouse couldn't move. She was pinned on her side. Panic filled her as the distinct odor of gasoline overwhelmed her nostrils. *The driver? Where is he?*

She couldn't see anything but the bottom of the doorframe that her face was uncomfortably pressed against. *I'm alive.* The thought only gave way to new concerns. She couldn't hear the driver. She didn't feel him move. There was a pressure on her right side from the driver's seat. It was collapsed down on her, making it difficult to breathe. A sense of claustrophobia crept in as she worked hard to create some space.

Mouse wiggled her right foot free. The release gave her hope. She snaked her body toward the tiny gap that her foot had found. Like an inchworm, she worked herself to the other side of the car. She took a deep lung full of air after escaping from the tightness of her pinned position.

Getting her bearings, she assessed the situation. She realized why the driver wasn't moving or making noise. His neck was twisted, and he was partially crammed between the steering wheel and the driver's door. A horrible sight. Mouse scanned for her exit.

Voices filled the air. Shrill panic-stricken motorists surrounded the damaged vehicle. She needed to get out. A strong hand grabbed mouse by her shoulders and pulled. Mouse managed to snag the strap of her backpack as she was hoisted out of the window.

The man who pulled her out stared at her in disbelief as if seeing a ghost.

"My God! Are you okay? We already called the police," the man said loudly, yelling over the noise.

He wore a brightly-colored Hawaiian shirt that seemed to oddly stand out against the mangled remnants of the vehicle that was Mouse's prison only moments before.

"Let's get you away from here."

"Wait!" Mouse yelled.

She dove back in through the opened window of the front passenger area. The man in the Hawaiian shirt and other do-gooders gave a simultaneous gasp of shock. Mouse popped back out a moment later, stuffing something into her backpack.

"I'm sorry about your father," the man said, assuming that Mouse had jumped back in to help him.

"Yeah," Mouse said, quietly.

No need to draw suspicion. *Look sad and walk away*.

"Follow me. The ambulance will be here soon," the man said.

Mouse trailed behind the red and yellow flowers that ordained the silky material of the shirt. He led her across the roadway that was now stopped in all directions.

"Take a seat here on the grass and I'll be right back with a bottle of water," the man said, patting her on the head.

The man hustled back to what Mouse assumed to be his station wagon. He reappeared with two bottles of water in hand. The man in the Hawaiian shirt paused as the condensation pooled rapidly around the plastic containers. He stared back toward the grassy median where the girl had just been. She was nowhere in sight. As if she'd vanished into the heat of the day.

Chapter 18

"How'd he sound?" Val asked, sounding genuinely concerned. Her need to psychoanalyze evident in situations like this.

"I don't know. Different. He didn't ask for my help, but it sounded like he wanted to," Declan said.

"He's family to us now, Deck. We do anything for family," Val said. She had a serious look in her mesmerizing eyes.

"I know that. And I guess that's why I'm so torn. Not sure what's the best move," Declan said. The confliction evident in his voice.

"I think I know who might be able to help with this decision," Val said, raising her eyebrow as she smiled coyly.

The reference to Nick's former partner, Izzy Martinez, was not lost on Declan. A missed opportunity for a relationship that Nick had passed on when he returned to Texas. It was a topic of conversation in the Enright house for several months after his departure.

"Maybe you're right. But I don't think he's been including her in his life as of late," Declan asserted.

"What makes you say that?" Val inquired.

"I ran into Izzy at a training session last month. She's moonlighting as a negotiator with the Bureau's SWAT and HRT groups."

Declan's unit crossed-trained regularly with their Crisis Negotiation Teams (CNT) so that communications and tactics were in sync.

"I asked her if she'd heard anything from Nick. Her face told the story. She seemed sad. Didn't really say much but hinted that it's been a while," Declan added.

"Maybe so, but I'm sure that he'd welcome a call from her. Call it a woman's intuition." Val loved talking relationships with Declan. She could sense his discomfort with the topic and thus made every effort to torment the man she loved. "I could call her for you if you'd prefer."

"No. This is something I should do. I want to hear her take on my impression of Nick's last call. It'll hopefully put my mind at ease," Declan said, softly.

Just then, Laney appeared in the kitchen. She stood silently and slowly swiveled her head from Mom and then over to her dad. Her small hand reached cautiously outward and gently intertwined with Declan's pinky. The delicate fingers of his four-year-old wrapped around his finger. Declan automatically began to softly caress the outside of her hand with his thumb. A routine connection that his daughter had created a few weeks ago after celebrating her fourth birthday. Declan felt that it was as calming for him as it was for her. Laney still only spoke on the rarest of occasions, but Val and Declan celebrated any form of communication from the daughter. They'd both developed adjusted parenting strategies since she was diagnosed with Autism.

"I'd hate to take off for Texas and leave you all alone with our wrecking crew. Especially, if I don't know what I'm getting myself into," Declan said.

Val was strong but the demands of their three young daughters were exhausting. It was exacerbated with the constant challenge of Laney's sudden meltdowns. Those moments were tough even when both parents were present.

Declan was a devout father and never put work in front of family, when possible. They'd adjusted to the sporadic schedule of being a member of the FBI's elite Hostage Rescue Team. His heroics in thwarting a devastating terrorist plot during the previous year had landed him some flexibility that others in his position didn't have. It also didn't hurt that he'd been decorated by the President himself.

She answered on the second ring.

"Hey, stranger! And what do I owe this honor?" Izzy asked. Her voice was a mixture of excitement and guarded inquisitiveness.

"I know. It was good seeing you at training. I wanted to touch base with you on a strange call I received," Declan said, cutting out the small talk.

"Call?" Izzy asked. "Him?"

"Yup," Declan said. She was quick on the uptake.

"Tell me what's got you worried," Izzy said.

"That's the thing. It was what he didn't say. I called him to give the update about the J's pizza takedown. He was evasive. Sounded like he wanted to tell me something or ask for my help. But he didn't." Declan heard the out-of-character discord. He attempted to clarify and continued, "It was something in his voice."

"I know you well enough to trust that gut instinct of yours. If you sensed that something was off, then I'm guessing you're right to be concerned." Izzy's voice trailed off.

"Maybe we'd get more if you reached out to him," Declan said, with some hesitancy.

A sigh and then a long pause before Izzy responded, "Maybe. I'm not sure but, if Nick is in some sort of trouble, then it's worth a shot."

"Thanks, Izzy. You're the best," Declan said, with genuine endearment.

"I wish he felt that way," Izzy said, softly. Then she hung up.

Izzy stared down at Nick's number, hovering above the call button. The hesitation frustrated her, but she knew why. It had taken a long time to bury the hope that Nick would call for her. That he would find a way to open up himself to her. And now she would look weak. But Declan's request trumped her personal misgivings.

Chapter 19

"This interruption better be worth it," the man in the expensive suit hissed into the phone.

He was a man of control. A man who was not a slave to the whims of others. The pager message was urgent. So, he'd made that call.

"Simon had an early retirement. The delivery was lost," the man on the other end said.

His voice was clear, and the message was delivered with a simple guise in the event that his boss was in earshot of someone outside of their circle.

"This is unacceptable. Notify Cain. I expect that this situation will be resolved by the end of my luncheon."

The man in the expensive suit relayed this with an eerie calm. The mention of Cain would express the seriousness of the situation. He hung up without waiting for a response. He returned to the ornate room and to the company seated around the secluded table.

"Senator Murdock, my apologies for the disruption. You know better than most the challenges of running a business."

"James, no need. Your work and charities are integral to our state. It gave me a chance to pitch your idea to Jerry," Murdock said, his thick mustache carried a remnant of the cheesecake that he'd just forked into his fleshy cheeks.

"Pastor Collins, I think that you will be the perfect person to endorse his border reform campaign. Your work with illegal immigrants has been amazing and will help humanize us to those opposing our cause," Jerry said. He continued, "I mean this is Texas and we're trying to stop the wall from going up. Nothing like swimming upstream."

"Please, just call me James. No titles necessary here. Just some friends trying to figure out how to help some people in need." Collins said, smiling broadly and exposing his perfect teeth.

Collins adjusted the silver cufflinks embossed with the symbol of the Saint Benedict Cross. His open collar gave him a casual air, but there was nothing casual about the man.

"How long has the package been out for delivery?" Cain asked.

He carried no detectable accent. His past had long since been erased. He was known only by the name given to him on the first day he came to work for the Pastor. Collins was the only living person that knew his real name. But it had been so long since he'd heard it uttered that he'd never reacted to its calling. His life changed when he met the religious man. His naming carried a reference to his beginnings, like that of his biblical namesake.

"Two hours." The man on the other end said, knowing why this was asked.

"Intact?" Cain asked.

"Yes. And mobile. Pacing indicates that travel is by foot." The directness of the man spoke to his awareness of his role. A relay of information. Nothing more.

"Send me the link. Updates to me only until I locate the package," Cain said.

He stood and drained the last remaining drops from his iced coffee. He left the payment on the table. The cash under his now empty cup flapped in the mid-afternoon breeze as he walked away from the bistro toward his silver Range Rover.

Chapter 20

The vibration alerted in his pocket distracted him from the conversation with Jones. Nick pulled his cell and stared at the incoming call. Jones was still talking in the background, postulating his theory on where the girl may have gone. Nick stopped listening. Atypical behavior but the caller had completely derailed his train of thought.

"Are you still here?" Jones chided.

"Yeah. Sorry," Nick answered, as if coming out of a trance.

"Take it if you need. No hurt feelings here," Jones said.

"No. I'll let it go to voicemail." Nick felt like he needed to add something more in the way of an explanation and continued, "Just a blast from the past."

"Well, thank God all my ex's live in Texas," Jones said, laughing at the play on the words of George Straight.

ı an ex. Well, not really. My former partner,"

stopped himself mid-sentence, realizing that the more he said the crazier he sounded. It didn't help that his cheeks were starting to flush.

"Well, don't get all embarrassed on my account," Jones said.

Like blood in the water, the heavyset investigator took this opportunity to rib his colleague.

"You're really loving this," Nick said. He smiled, lowered his head and conceded defeat. "Don't worry. At some point, I will fill you in on all the interesting details of my personal life."

"I can't wait." Jones laughed, giving Nick a playful rap on the back.

"So, back to the girl. Car?" Nick asked.

"That'd be my guess. Maybe she flagged someone down. The bus stop is down the street, but the track didn't seem to go in that direction," Jones said.

"Let's head back to see if we can get some more from Anaya," Nick said.

"Sounds like a plan. She sent me a text and is back at her office. Also, I checked in with the boss and it doesn't seem like any of the girls from the motel are ready to talk." Jones said.

Nick nodded. He noticed that Jones sounded proud to make the claim that Anaya Patel had sent him a text message.

"She's really good at her job. I've worked with her before. I've reached out to her for assistance on these types of cases. She's got a real knack for 'em," Jones said, giving another boost to the social worker's abilities.

"Is there more to this endorsement than job skills?" Nick said, with a hint of playfulness.

This was the second time that Jones had acted out of character at the mention of Anaya. Maybe there something more to the friendship between the detective and the social worker. Nick seized the opportunity to return the favor. It was the least he could do after the barrage of innuendoes that Jones showered him with after he ignored Izzy's call.

"Very funny! Don't be trying to use your legendary powers of observation on me," Jones said.

Now, with the roles reversed it was Jones's cheeks that reddened. Nick smiled at his small victory.

Anaya Patel's office was cool and smelled of lavender. She had an oil diffuser and the small tea light warmed the white ceramic bowl suspended above, casting the fragrance into the air. It added to the comfort of the room. Nick pictured that the victims and families that she met here were probably put at ease by the simple ambiance. Nick found it strange that the most recent visitor was so quick to leave.

"No luck?" Anaya said.

She nervously drummed her fingertips on the open file on her desk. Her eyes tightened in hopeful anticipation. A genuine concern in her voice.

"I wish we had something more. As of right now, she's in the wind," Jones said.

"Maybe we'll locate a surveillance camera in the area that caught her getting into a vehicle. Fingers crossed we might get lucky and be able to grab a make and model of the car. If luck is really on our side, then we'll get a license plate," Nick said, trying to reassure that more efforts were still going to be made.

"I put a broadcast out to patrol. Units have her physical description. I've already sent the still shot of her from the 7-11 to command so that officers will have the digital image to assist in identifying her. Public Affairs will create a media broadcast to run on this evening's news," Jones injected.

"I wish there was more that I could do," Anaya said, sitting behind her small, tidy desk as her nervous ritual of tapping her fingers on a notepad in front of her began again.

"So, no name? No idea where she came from? And no idea where she was going?" Nick asked.

"No. Well, she did tell me her name. Or at least what she goes by," Anaya said.

She pursed her lips, making a face that was somewhere between a smile and frown.

Anaya then added, "Mouse. She told me to call her Mouse."

Chapter 21

The red dot on his screen hadn't moved in forty minutes. He was still an hour out of the city. He'd left Dallas after receiving the call. The priority of the orders caused him to end his previous task abruptly. *The Hand's work is never done*, he'd thought. The Range Rover hummed quietly as he traversed south on the interstate. Cain always kept the speed within plus or minus three miles per hour of the posted limit. No need to draw unwanted attention. Blend and move. A shadow in the darkness.

The infectious words of the Pastor piped through the speakers. It was the only thing Cain listened to when inside the vehicle. He had a voluminous collection of CDs containing the preacher's sermons. Each word was scripted to him and applied directly to his life. As if God himself had whispered these great things in his ear. It was the Pastor's voice had called out to him in that room years ago as a child. That room was filled with horrors that now seemed more like an old nightmare rather than a memory.

The Pastor had been his salvation, saving him from the demons and bringing him into the light.

The Heathen was probably eating. Or just hiding. It did not matter. With each passing mile marker, Cain tingled with the excitement in the anticipation of what was to come. He relished the opportunity to serve. And the Heathen would soon pay for upsetting the Pastor. It didn't matter the age, gender or race of the Heathen because he'd been taught that the devil can take many forms.

Once Mouse was far enough away from the site of the car crash, she found the shade of a tree and sat. The dump of adrenaline during her escape had subsided and now left her exhausted. The tough Saint Augustine grass poked at her pants as she adjusted into a more comfortable position, ensuring that no fire ant mounds were underneath.

She pulled her legs to her chest and wrapped her arms around her shins as if giving herself a hug. Mouse let her forehead rest on her knees and she closed her eyes. Sleep was not the intention and she knew that would be a long way off. She just needed a minute to reset and clear her mind of recent events.

She had two maps in her backpack that she'd purchased from the convenience store. One was of Austin and the other was of the Continental United States. She pulled that latter out and spread it across the dry grass.

Slightly refreshed by her respite in the shade, she navigated her fingers around the map's surface finding Texas and then isolating Austin. It was an overwhelming network of roads leading in and out of the state's capital. A bigger city than she'd expected. *Easy to get lost in.*

She straightened her back and then slowly shifted her head from side to side. The tension of the crash caused her muscles to ache. It would only worsen as time passed. With her neck cocked to one side, something caught her eye in the near distance. She examined the sign and immediately knew her next move.

The emergency vehicles working the crash scene were close enough that the whine of their sirens floated in the heavy mid-morning air. People would be looking for her. Some of those people would want to hurt her. Others would want to send her back. Both options were unacceptable. Forward was the only way. Her promise to her mother to keep.

A Greyhound Bus depot was just beyond where she sat. The billboard advertisement rising high above the low trees pitched cheap fares to destinations anywhere across the country. Mouse had a little over four hundred and fifty dollars. Donations of the bad men from the box truck. She no longer had the knife. The nice lady with the office bed had taken that from her during her short visit. That knife had served its purpose but also carried with it the terrible memory of the old man's death. She was glad to be rid the tainted blade. It didn't matter anyway, now that she had the driver's gun tucked at the bottom of her backpack.

A weapon is only as deadly as the person who holds it. Her father's words. Strange but true.

Mouse's finger slowly drifted up the large unfolded map of the United States. She moved away from Austin and stopped when it hit the blue water of the Michigan lakes.

She wanted to start her new life as far away from where this journey began. And she liked water.

One of her only memories of her father that didn't included his challenging survival training was that of the fishing trips they took together. He was a different man when the two would sit along the bank of the Rio Grande. It was the only time that she recalled seeing him smile. *Maybe he's smiling now at seeing the result of all his hard lessons?*

She looked around the lake area, scanning the map for the right destination. Her father had taught her how to read a map, using the legend and scale to interpret the details. He explained that the size of the letters on a map indicated the population and size of the city. She wanted to find one that was not too big and not too small. Just like Goldilocks, she wanted to find one that was just right. Her finger stopped. Pidgeon, Michigan. *Funny to name a place after a bird.* It sounded like a good enough place for her begin her new life.

Content with her decision, she reached into her bag and pulled out a bottle of water and an apple. The slight bruising on the red fruit's exterior caused by the turbulent crash did little to slow her consumption. She ravenously devoured it. The fruit's juice trickled down the little girl's chin.

To an onlooker she looked like any other kid, but Mouse was anything but ordinary.

Chapter 22

"I don't know about this. Don't seem right," the grizzled man said, slurring as he spoke.

His breath, a potent combination of cigarettes and booze, filled the air around his face. In the heaviness of the day's heat, the stench enveloped him like a blanket.

"Please. My grandmother is dying, and I need to get home to see her," Mouse said.

Her voice sweetened, giving a softness that made her seem younger and more innocent than she was. Her eyes pleaded into the man's bloodshot stare. The jaundiced coloring of the man's skin gave him a sickly look. The cruelties of his affliction evident.

"Hmmm. How'm I gonna know you ain't runnin' away. Con-terr-abootin' to a minor's de-linq-uency is bad." The man's limited education was readily apparent to the girl. His intoxication added to his dimwittedness.

"I wrote down on this slip of paper where I need to go. Find out how much and I'll give you that plus a twenty for your trouble," Mouse said.

A twinkle in the man's eyes at the prospect of the money. And she had a pretty good guess what he would spend it on.

He greedily took the slip of paper from the girl and walked slowly into the bus station ticketing area, stumbling only once on the lip of the curb. The drunken man was doing his best impression of a sober person. A tough role for him to play. But as far as bum actors go, he'd be in the running for an Oscar.

Mouse stood out of view from the glass doors of the ticket office. She bit the inside of her lip. A nervous habit that became more frequent in recent months. She didn't want anyone to see her exchange with the homeless man. Using him as her go-between had its potential for failure. She released the pressure on her lip when he returned a few minutes later.

"It's gonna be hundered-sixty-one dullars. But ain't gonna getcha as fur as ya want. Some place called Sag-in-naw," the man said, smiling awkwardly at his success. A gesture that displayed the gaps in-between his few remaining stained teeth.

Mouse stepped back from the man and pulled out her map. It took her a moment of searching before she found Saginaw. *Close enough.* She'd figure a way to get to the water, to Pidgeon, once she was there. She returned the map to the pack's interior.

"Deal," Mouse said, turning away from the man as she reached into the zipper pocket.

She didn't want him to see the wad of money. Or the black handgun resting at the bottom. Her hand pressed out toward the man. He took the cash and looked back at her.

"I put a little extra just in case. You can keep whatever bit of change is left over. I will give you your twenty when you come back," Mouse said, assertively.

The man's filthy fingers rubbed the bills together, calculating its value. Mouse could tell that it had been a long time since this man had held so much. She worried that the man would try to run off with the cash, but she had a keen eye for people and saw some good in him. He didn't want to initially help because he thought that he might be contributing to the delinquency of a minor. Bad people don't worry about stuff like that. And in a worst-case scenario, if she'd read him wrong, then it would be to his loss. She would have no difficulty running him down and retrieving what was hers.

The man walked away with the crumpled cash in his right hand and disappeared into the station again. He moved a little faster this time. The pep in his step at the prospect of having twenty dollars in his pocket proved to be all the motivation he needed.

The money was replaced by the white gleam reflecting off the ticketing paperwork. She hadn't noticed it before, but the man walked with a limp. He leaned to one side as he swiveled his hip forward with each step of his return. The movement was more pronounced due to the unbalance created by his intoxication. Mouse already had palmed the twenty-dollar bill. The exchange would be quick.

"I hope your gramma is okay," the man said as he swapped the tickets for his wage.

"Umm. Yeah. Thanks." Mouse glanced at the paperwork in her hand.

She walked away from the man. It took a few minutes of walking to rid herself of the man's odor. His stink had permeated her clothes. The breeze helped to wick away its remnants.

Mouse went back to her tree. Her temporary shelter. She sat and closely evaluated the itinerary. *Damn.* The bus didn't leave until tomorrow morning at 4:30 am. She'd need to find a place for the night. The Holiday Inn that was located directly across the street from the bus depot would work. *A lot better than under a tree.*

"What did he say? No shit? Keep him there. I'm on the way," Jones said.

He was animated, grabbing at his notepad and stuffing a couple pens into his breast pocket.

"What've we got?" Nick asked, startled by the detective's sudden burst of energy.

"Patrol's working a crash on I35. A witness said there was a girl in the car. She disappeared before units arrived on scene," Jones said, speaking in rapid-fire succession.

"Disappeared?" Anaya chimed in, grabbing a file from the top of her desk and slipping it under her arm. "Is it her?"

"Not sure. She's nowhere to be found," Jones said. Concern in his voice as he continued, "They're keeping the witness on location for us. I'd rather hear it from the horse's mouth."

"Let's move," Nick said, already in stride for the door.

All in good time. *Patience is the virtue that yields the biggest promise.* Words from the Pastor. Teachings from the Master. He was closing in on the area of the red dot. The screen mapping his trip zoomed in as he lessened his position to within ten miles of the blip. Cain manipulated the map further with his fingers, trying to get his bearings. He hated technology. But the Pastor told him that it was needed and so he used it.

The Heathen was somewhere just off the interstate. He knew better than to drive directly to that location. He would find a place nearby and approach on foot. Best to observe before acting. From the information provided thus far, it appeared that the Heathen had managed to escape twice. Cain would not allow the same to happen to him. *I'm the Right Hand. I carry God's sword. And when directed, I swing it hard upon His enemy.*

In background, the Pastor ranted about the injustice of man's indignation toward the will of God. His words kissed the ears of Cain and soothed his bubbling anguish. He longed to see the praise in the Pastor's eyes after he completed the task. It was all the reward he needed. It was the only fuel that fed his soul.

Chapter 23

"Show me exactly where she was last standing," Jones said.

He was terser and his normally laidback mannerisms were gone. His worry for the girl's well-being was spilling over. This is how so many cops lost the balance between the job and life. And right now Jones could think of nothing else except finding this missing girl.

Anaya listened to the description given by the man in the Hawaiian shirt and was convinced that the girl from the crash was Mouse. She nervously scanned the area, hoping to spot her.

"Here. Right here," the man said, using his arms to show the area where the girl last stood. He resembled an airline stewardess directing passengers to the emergency exits.

"This must be your guy. Got a county car pulling up now," Nick called out, over the noise emergency crews.

"Damn, you're fast," Jones said, as Rusty Harrison stepped out of his Crown Victoria. He was wearing olive drab fatigue pants and a light tan t-shirt.

"I told you I live close and would be ready for your call," Rusty said, smiling at the opportunity to help.

"Alright then. Let me give you the rundown," Jones said, throwing in a little twang to punctuate the sentence. "She was in that mangled sedan and then was last seen standing over there."

"She walked away from that?" Rusty asked.

His eyes widened in disbelief, the shock of a seasoned lawman that had seen the resulting devastation of a crash like this.

"Unbelievable, isn't it? This girl has one hell of a guardian angel," Nick said to the pair.

"You've got that right. Hopefully it will be enough to keep her safe until we find her," Jones said, staring back at the wreckage.

"Let me get started." Rusty said.

Rusty looked at the FBI agents tall, lean physique, sizing up his fitness level and then added, "Nick, do you want to run the track with me?"

"I'll do my best to keep up," Nick said, modestly.

"Anaya and I will follow in the Jetta. Windows up and air on," Jones said, laughing at his own joke.

"Acclimate my friend," Nick retorted, as he broke into a light jog behind Rusty with Jasper at the helm.

Cain stood in front of the Gold's Gym located along a small strip of businesses. He was not dressed in workout attire. The patrons entering and exiting the establishment wearing tank tops and shorts gave him wearisome glances as they passed.

His Range Rover was parked several rows away from where he stood. He wore rip-stop cargo pants and a lightweight button-up polo. The untucked shirt concealed his weaponry, but he wasn't concerned if they were seen. This was Texas and the open-carry law enabled him to display a firearm without a second glance from most of the citizenry.

He watched the Heathen as she meandered about the parking lot of hotel. She was small. *But evil comes in all sizes.* In times like these he reminded himself to think of the snake in the Garden of Eden and how it forever changed man. And now, great men like the Pastor were forced to fix the devil's doing.

The Heathen was ducked low between a couple of parked cars as if tying her shoe. She'd been holding in that position for several minutes. Cain watched intently, trying to understand what she was up to. Then it became clear.

A person passed by her wheeling a small suitcase. The guest slid his key into the slot by the door and went in through the side entrance of the Holiday Inn. The Heathen stood and followed, moving quickly to catch the door just before closing. *Tricky girl.*

The hallway of the Holiday Inn was thirty degrees cooler than outside. To Mouse, it was as if she'd walked into a meat locker. She shivered as her body adjusted to the variance. Tiny goosebumps prickled along her skin. The man whom she'd followed in never turned around. His indifference meant that he didn't notice her.

To be small is a gift. Use it to your advantage, her father had said to her.

She navigated the hallway until she saw her opportunity. A maid's bin was parked outside a room on the right side of the hallway. It wasn't long before a heavy-set dark-skinned woman strutted out of the propped opened door. She wore a uniform shirt with the hotel's moniker embroidered above her ample breasts. The uniform's material worked hard to contain her large frame, like a dam holding back a reservoir's water.

The worker grabbed two new trash bags and re-entered the room. Mouse moved quickly. She walked by the door and peered in as she passed. The maid was bent over in the corner with her large backside to the door. Mouse peeked in and noticed that all of the bathroom towels had been replaced and the area tidied. Confident that the maid had finished in the bathroom, Mouse slipped inside.

Mouse scampered into the modest bathroom, climbing into the white porcelain tub. The shower curtain was heavy and to her advantage, not transparent. Laying down she slowly drew that curtain closed. The cheap plastic hooks slid across the metallic bar until she was satisfied that her small frame was covered by the heavy plastic.

She waited. The heavy maid hummed a tune. The sound of it reminded Mouse of her mother when she used to hang the laundry from the line outside their small house, humming and smiling away the labors. Mouse closed her eyes and listened contentedly, allowing a momentary peace to replace the frantic morning.

The bathroom light clicked off. The door to the hallway closed and with it so did the lyrical hum of the cleaning lady. Mouse slumped deeper into the tub allowing the coolness of its surface to caress her hot skin.

In the cramped space of the tub, with her backpack still on, Mouse drifted off into the deepest sleep she'd had in   weeks.

Chapter 24

The door clicked, and a flicker of green indicated that the key card had disengaged the lock. The handle pressed down and the seal released with a suction sound. The room was dark, but the sunlight fought through the pulled blinds, providing enough light to guide his entry.

He moved heel-to-toe across the carpet into the bedroom. The sheets were undisturbed. Standing in the silence, a faint sound trickled out from the bathroom. *Snoring?* He moved quickly but carefully, ensuring that he would limit her surprise. No need for screams.

She hadn't heard the door open, but something caused her to wake. *How long was I out?* Impossible to tell in the confines of the tub.

Someone was in the room. No doubt about it. No lights were turned on. Not a guest. Not a maid. Mouse exhaled slowly, adjusting her eyes to the dark. She needed to get the gun. It was still resting at the bottom of her backpack. She gingerly slipped free her shoulder, working hard not to bang against the tub. Every movement she made seemed to be amplified a thousand times by the tub's porcelain basin.

Mouse's lower lip quivered as she tugged at the zipper, moving its teeth down the side of the backpack a few grooves at a time. Her fingers trembled. She was mad at herself for falling asleep. She'd let her guard down and now she was at a disadvantage. The footsteps on the tile floor of the bathroom startled her.

Abandoning her effort to move silently, she yanked at the zipper and shoved her hand deep into the bag's opening. Her small fingers finding purchase of the rough grip of the pistol as the curtain whipped away, exposing her curled figure.

"Mouse?" The tall man said, his voice firm but kind.

She looked up at him. Her right hand gripped around the butt of the gun, but she hesitated in removing it. The mention of her name had derailed her train of thought and her hand remained buried in the bag.

"Mouse? That's what Anaya said to call you. Are you okay?" Nick asked.

He noted that she was aptly named. Half-tucked in the empty tub, she looked so small. Delicate. But her eyes were not. She stared at him intensely and he could tell that she was rapidly assessing him.

Mouse nodded. Hand still in the backpack, unflinching.

"Clear. She's in here. In the bathroom," Nick called out, turning his head slightly but not looking away from the girl. Afraid that if he took his eyes off her for an instant then she would disappear.

"My goodness, you had me worried," Anaya said, appearing behind Nick's broad shoulders.

Mouse transitioned her focus to the social worker and released her grip, letting the gun settle back to the bottom of the sack submerged under the pile of PowerBars.

"Let me help you up," Anaya Patel said, edging her way around the FBI agent's chiseled frame.

She placed her left hand on the center of his back as she passed him. She felt the taut muscles of the agent and was distracted for a fleeting moment by the contact.

"I'll step out and give you two a moment," Nick said, knowing that most girls in Mouse's circumstance did not usually take to interactions with adult males. No telling the trauma in her past and he didn't want to add to it.

"Mouse you had me so worried," Anaya said. She didn't admonish the child and continued without awaiting a response from the girl, "Why did you leave? I only want to help you."

"You can't." Mouse's tone was flat.

She wanted nothing more than to snuggle on the cot in Anaya's office and sleep for days. But she wouldn't be safe there. Mouse wasn't sure if she'd ever be safe again. The man in the car had found her quickly. More would come. She was sure of that.

This is bad. The police have found the Heathen first. The Pastor would be angry at his failings. Hopefully, he would allow him the opportunity to redeem himself.

Cain pulled out a small folding pocket knife as he walked back to the Range Rover. The handle, made of a white bone, seemed brighter in the late afternoon sun. It was etched with the Pastor's words, *Only with God's Hand can evil be cut out.*

Cain rolled his sleeve past his elbow and dug the blade into his thick bicep. The release of blood gave him peace and he could feel his pulse rate slow. The droplets rolled down the tanned flesh of his arm and fell to the dry earth at his feet. Cain squinted, casting an intense gaze as the small Heathen exited the hotel and entered the rear door of Volkswagen.

They passed without ever looking in his direction. He remained unseen. The Pastor told Cain that he'd been given a shroud of invisibility. *Heathens could not bear witness to the Hand of God.*

Only in those moments of terror had he ever revealed himself. *The Heathen's time was coming and she would soon know his face.*

Chapter 25

"Hi," Nick said, answering his phone. He couldn't allow it to go unanswered again.

He slapped his hand against his head and rolled his eyes. He was mad at himself that after several months without speaking to her that *Hi* was all he could muster. *Epic failure.*

"It's been a while. Everything alright?" Izzy asked. The impatience clearly etched in her voice stemmed from an equal combination of anger and worry.

"Yeah. I'm fine," Nick mumbled. *Oh, this is painful. Why can't I talk to the one person I trusted above all others?*

"How's your mom? Is she adjusting to her new surroundings?" Izzy asked, genuinely.

"It's touch and go. They moved her to a more isolated section due to some recent outbursts," Nick said.

He felt a lump in his throat. He hadn't spoken about his mother to anyone as of late. He didn't have anyone out west that he felt close enough with to share that side of his life. Izzy had been that person and he'd effectively cut her out.

"Oh Nick, I'm so sorry," Izzy said, putting aside her frustration.

Nick was silent. He knew that if he spoke he might fall apart. A man not comfortable with outwardly expressing his emotions, he fought back against the whirlwind of feelings. He hung back from the others, leaning against the trunk of his Jetta as Jones and Anaya accompanied the small girl through the doors of the Child Protective Services headquarters. The heat off the car's black exterior caused him to pop up immediately. He drifted over to the shade provided by a cluster of small trees.

"What's new with you?" Nick said, redirecting the conversation away from the emotional landmine of his mother's condition.

"Not much. Same old stuff here." Izzy noted that Nick was deflecting and did not press. She smiled at the sound of her old partner's voice, even if it was under the awkwardness of the current conversation. "I saw Deck a while back. He's good. I think he's having fun kicking in doors and hunting bad guys."

"It's what he does best," Nick said, with a chuckle.

"He told me that you two talked earlier," Izzy said, pausing long enough to prepare for her next question, "What's going on with you?"

"What do you mean? I can't just call an old friend and say hello?" Nick asked, defensively.

He knew that he'd just opened himself to an onslaught from Izzy, regretting the words as soon as they left his mouth.

"Call an old friend, huh? How about me, Nick? Ever think of picking up the damn phone and calling me?" Izzy snapped.

Normally she was the epitome of calm and so the anger in her voice caught him off guard. But he knew that she had a right to feel that way. That night together in the hotel room still replayed in his dreams. Hearing her voice now, only tormented him further. It'd been the reason that he'd broken off communication months ago.

"Sorry," Nick muttered. It was all he could come up with. There was so much he wanted to say but he held back.

"That's the best you can do? Sorry?" Izzy was breathing heavily through the phone as she added, "I was there for you. Always had been. I thought we had something real. Maybe something lasting. Then, out of the blue, you up and leave."

"I know. I just…" Nick fumbled with the words.

"You don't know shit! I waited. Months I waited. And nothing. No call. Not even a weak-ass text message. Nothing!" Izzy unloaded. Her words were spoken through grit teeth.

"You're right. It was a shitty thing. You didn't deserve it. You deserve better," Nick said, softly.

"That's the first thing you've got right so far. And that's what I decided too! I moved on. Hard as it was. But I moved on!" Izzy's initial assault had passed, and her voice began to soften again.

Nick felt sick to his stomach. It had been seven months since he'd left Connecticut. Since he'd left Izzy. And he hadn't made one attempt to contact her over the last three. Well, that wasn't entirely true. He'd taken out his phone and stared at her number multiple times a day since their last conversation, but he never made the call.

"Is there anything that you want to say to me?" Izzy asked.

Her frustration returned with his silence.

"I'm not sure what to say," Nick said.

"Then I'm not going to be the one to tell you. It doesn't work that way."

Izzy had walled herself up again, shielding her heart from Nick's inability to commit. She delivered the final blow, "His name is Bill and he's a good man."

"Bureau guy?" Nick asked.

He was woozy at the thought of another man touching Izzy.

"No way. Never again. You were my first and last in that department," Izzy said.

Her edginess dissipated slowly with a sigh.

"Met him at the rehab facility when I was recovering from my ankle injury. Which, by the way, is much better. Thanks for asking."

Nick realized that he hadn't checked on her. The last time they talked she was still on light duty and using a cane to assist her mobility. She'd saved his life and he'd failed to look in on her recovery.

He made a meager offering, "I suck. What can I say?"

"Water under the bridge," Izzy responded.

"I wish that I could go back and do things over. Ya know? Do things right," Nick said, continuing his weak attempt at rectifying their past.

"That's not why I called. I'm not calling to rehash our failed relationship," Izzy said.

"Why then?" Nick asked, embarrassed by the direction this conversation had taken.

"Declan called me. He was concerned. Thought maybe I'd have better luck figuring out what's going on with you," Izzy said.

Her voice returned to normal. The hostility seemed to have vanished as quickly as it had come. Like an afternoon rainstorm in the summer.

"But I didn't say anything," Nick said, more defensively than he should've.

"It wasn't anything you said. More how you said it," Izzy said, prodding at Nick's aloofness.

"Hmm. He's a good read of people," Nick said.

"So, what's the deal?" Izzy said.

Her patience at this game of cat and mouse was waning.

"Nothing. Just a case I'm working. Bad one. I guess none of these crimes are ever good, but this feels worse. Bigger. I guess," Nick said.

His mind thought back to the girls in the motel. The small child by the graffiti wall. And Mouse.

"You sound shook. What can we do to help?" Izzy asked.

Nick pulled the phone away from his ear. He was blown away by his old partner's willingness to help. Especially, after he'd left her when she'd needed him most. Now she was ready to jump in and help. Isabella Martinez was the definition of loyal.

"Nick, are you still with me?" Izzy asked after his latest inject of silence.

"Sorry. Yes. I'm good. I've got this. Didn't mean to spook you guys. I was just a little overwhelmed. Nothing I can't handle," Nick said, regaining his composure.

"Well, if that changes then you know how to reach me," Izzy said.

Her voice flat. The disappointment evident.

"Yeah, I know. Thanks for looking out," Nick said and then added, "Good luck with Bill. I hope things work out."

Nick wished he could've stuffed a sock in his mouth. *Why the hell would he wish her well with another guy?*

"Okay," Izzy muttered, awkwardly.

The quiet that followed was only seconds, but to Nick it was an eternity.

"Take care of yourself," Izzy said, dejected.

The phone call ended with a click. Nick pocketed the phone and walked into the main lobby. The cool air of the building's interior did little to ebb his burning desire to undo that last conversation.

Chapter 26

"Thank God for Rusty and Jasper!" Jones said.

He was smiling as he sat on the corner of Anaya's desk. His ample rump came close to knocking over the green reading lamp that cast its subdued light on the stack of precariously balanced files.

"That's for sure," Nick said, rejoining the group. "I never noticed before, but your desk might be as bad as his."

Nick looked at Anaya, while thumbing in the direction of Jones. A big grin formed on his face.

"Great minds think alike, buddy," Jones laughed.

An ease settled over the group as the return of the girl gave hope to a seemingly desperate investigation. The girl sat slumped in the wooden chair positioned directly in front of the desk. Her toes stretched touching the floor and she nervously swiveled the seat from side to side. Her arms folded and head down. Mouse looked as if she were sitting in front of the principal with her parents standing in judgment. Although, Anaya's delicate face and deep dark eyes held none of the trademark signs of the school administrators that Nick had faced during his adolescence. If the situation wasn't so serious it would've made a great Norman Rockwell moment.

"What am I going to do with you?" Anaya said.

She was kind but not weak in her presentation to the child. An undercurrent of firmness resonated in her voice.

Mouse peered up at the social worker through her straight black hair that was flopped over her face. It was as if she were peering from behind a dark veil. Even under the web of hair, Mouse's eyes shone brightly. Anaya saw the spark. It's probably what's kept her alive through this ordeal. There was a fire inside of this girl. A natural toughness that Anaya recognized. She recognized it because she'd had deployed the same to survive her own challenge years before.

"I can't protect you if you keep disappearing," Anaya said, filling the void created by the unresponsive child.

"Who's the guy in the car?" Jones interjected.

The drawl was back but his tone easygoing. Not the gruffness he used on the street.

Mouse did not look at the detective. Nick knew that it was common for victims to avoid eye contact with authority figures. Especially when those figures happened to be males. She maintained her passive avoidance.

"We want to help but you've got to tell us somethin' hun," Jones said, pressing the girl a bit harder. Dropping in the drawl for added effect.

"Did you know him?" Anaya said, hoping to offer up some assistance by rephrasing the question.

Nick said nothing. He watched and listened. It wouldn't be productive for him to speak. The sign of a seasoned investigator is knowing when to use silence.

Mouse looked down. And then an almost imperceptive movement of her head. She slowly shook from side to side. Had he not been watching intently, Nick would have missed the girl's first attempt at communication with the group.

Jones's observant eye caught it too and he responded, "So you didn't know the guy? Then why'd he pick you up?"

"Did you ask for a ride from the man?" Anaya said.

Nick watched Jones and Anaya transition the lead while questioning the girl. It was obvious from the synchronous questioning that they'd deployed this tactic in the past. It was a very watered-down version of good cop/bad cop.

Mouse shook her head again. This time the movement was more noticeable. A sign that she was becoming more comfortable with the people in the room. An indication that a connection was being made. Nick evaluated body language with as much scrutiny as he did the spoken word.

"So, you didn't know him? And you didn't ask for a ride? Then how'd you end up in the car?" Jones said, looking for some answer that would clear the mystery.

Nick caught Jones's attention and gestured toward the door with a cock of his head, indicating that he wanted to talk outside the room. Jones registered the request and stood up from the desk. The two slipped out and closed the door, leaving Anaya alone with the girl.

"So, she is on the run and happens to get picked up by a guy she doesn't know. Then the guy ends up crashing and dying while she runs away again," Nick said, quietly.

"Well, what are we missing?" Jones asked, running his fingers through his thinning hairline.

"You and I both know that something's off here. She may not have known him, but there was definitely a reason she got in that car. There has to be some link," Nick said. His mind raced to connect the dots.

"I've got it," Jones said.

Without explaining, he reentered the room. Anaya was speaking quietly but Jones in his haste interrupted.

"You didn't know him, but you know who he works for?"

"Yes," Mouse said.

Her voice was low but what she lacked in volume she made up for in conviction. Mouse twisted slightly in her seat so that she could direct her answer to the rotund detective.

"I'll be damned. She speaks!" Jones exclaimed.

"Where is she now?" The Pastor asked.

His voice was steady, but the lack of inflection worried Cain.

"The Heathen is at the Child Protective Services building. I'm down the street," Cain said.

He tried to show confidence, hoping to demonstrate to the Pastor that he was worthy of another opportunity. His right hand rotated the pocket knife. He registered the embossed lettering as his thumb caressed over it.

Tempted to relieve his tension as he awaited the Pastor's judgment.

"You are my Hand. If you falter, then so shall I. The Lord has spoken to me and you shall be granted another pass," the Pastor said.

Cain bathed himself in the words. His eyes watered. Another opportunity given. A second chance at redemption.

"Remember, my son, those who stand in the way of you are defying God's will. Bring the Heathen forth so that she may be judged!" The Pastor boomed.

These last words echoed through the phone as if standing on the pulpit. The call then abruptly ended.

Cain felt an exhilaration. *Service is its own reward*. He vowed that he would not fail again.

Chapter 27

His fingers pressed deep into the neoprene surface and his back straight. Downward dog seemed so simple now but had eluded him for the first few months. He'd watched Val slip into the position with ease but every time he saw his reflection in the glass doors of the bookcase in their living room he looked nothing like her. It took time for his body to find the feel of the positions. But once he did it unlocked something inside him.

Enya blared through his earbuds, carrying him away as he embraced his ritual of sequential movements. Typically, Declan did his yoga before anyone was awake. He'd found the sweet spot in his life was 4:00 am. A time before the chaos of the day had begun, but sometimes even his early morning schedule went awry as this Sunday morning had. Because of the raid on J's Pizza shop earlier he was now trying to fit his routine in while his girls were eating their lunch. The giggles coming from the kitchen were as soothing to him as the music in his ears. He smiled.

The phone vibrated twice on the floor in front of him, indicating a text message. Declan did not like being a slave to the phone, but his role on the Bureau's HRT dictated otherwise. The unit remained on an on-call status. And they'd been busy hunting any connections to The Seven. Luckily, today's mission took place in Hartford, enabling Declan to get home early after he wrapped up his debrief.

He glanced at the name that accompanied the message. Dropping to his knees, he ended his routine and picked up the phone to read it.

Izzy: *Call me.*

Declan sat on the mat and spoke softly into the phone, trying hard not alert the children of the interruption to his routine. He knew if they thought he was done his workout, then they would come barreling in to play.

"Hey there. So, what'd you find out?" Declan said in almost a whisper, tucking the phone between his shoulder and ear.

"You were right. Something is definitely off with him," Izzy said.

"Did he give any indication as to what it might be?" Declan asked, sounding concerned.

"He said it was related to a case. Something bad, but he gave no details. He was very aloof," Izzy said.

Her frustration bled through the receiver in the form of exaggerated series of sighs.

"That's weird. We chased a damn terrorist around the country and Nick never seemed phased. I wonder what's got him so messed up," Declan said.

"Me too. He did tell me that he had unfinished business in Texas. Never let on to what it was or what he meant by it," Izzy said.

Izzy paused for a moment. She'd considered what he'd meant by those words he'd said to her before leaving Connecticut. *Unfinished business.* She'd always thought it might've had something to do with his ex-wife but was too afraid to ask. She never thought that it might be related to work.

Izzy continued, "To be honest, he always held back a bit when he talked about his time out west. Ya know? Kind of guarded."

"Hmm. So, what's the play?" Declan asked, eager to help his friend.

"Not sure. If you're around later let's meet up for a quick bite. I always think more clearly with a little food in my belly," Izzy suggested.

"Absolutely. There's a great little spot here on Main Street. How does Village Pizza sound?" Declan asked.

"Sounds like a plan. I'll see you at six. If that works?" Izzy asked.

"Six it is. See you then," Declan said.

He turned on his music and resumed his routine, picking up where he'd left off. But it was too late. His three girls appeared before him, smiling their toothy smiles. The workout over, Declan conceded to their silent request for play. Laney stood off to the side and watched as Ripley and Abigail climbed onto his back.

The three stared at the small girl. Their eyes squinting and peering at her, like mentalists trying to see into her mind.

All done with the intent to gauge how to best help her circumstances.

"You're a real challenge for us. You are a flight risk, so we can't put you in a traditional setting. You'd disappear from any family we put you with and there is no way that I'm putting you in a group home. Not after the ordeals you've been through. And it's all made worse by the fact that you're in danger," Anaya said. Her words were spoken to the girl but directed at the group.

"She's going to need protection. A round-the-clock kind of deal. I don't think your agency is capable of providing that," Jones said.

Anaya's head pulled back and her brow furrowed. Jones realized that he may have come off a bit harsher than intended and quickly interjected, "No offense meant. Hell, I don't even know if we'd be able to keep this one safe."

"None taken. I agree. She is in need of a protective detail and a place to hide out until we can figure this thing out," Anaya said.

"We don't even know who's after her. That would be a nice place to start, but one thing is for certain I don't think they're going to give up the hunt," Nick said, tension in his voice.

"Agreed," Jones said.

Jones rubbed his belly subconsciously. Hunger always came to him in moments of stress. Maybe that's why he'd let his pants out twice since becoming a member of the sex crimes unit. Each case serious and each victim important.

"She could stay at my place. I've got a spare bedroom," Nick offered.

He smirked at the awkwardness of the invitation. He'd never taken in a victim before and knew it would definitely violate some protocols. But working outside of agency directives was not something new to him.

Mouse adjusted in her seat, twisting her body so that she could make eye contact with the FBI agent. She said nothing. Her face was unreadable.

"I'll stay with you too," Anaya said, too eagerly.

Her eyes glanced around the room, trying to determine if the others had noticed the trace of enthusiasm of her comment. Blushing, her light brown cheeks took on the color of an autumn leaf.

Anaya continued, "I just meant that I think that Mouse would be more comfortable if I were to remain with her."

Mouse nodded but didn't look away from Nick. She was still evaluating him. She stared directly into his light blue eyes, unblinking as though peering into his soul.

"So, I guess I'm the odd man out," Jones said, with a laugh.

"You're welcome to come too but, I'm going to be honest, either you or Anaya are going to be playing rock-paper-scissors for the couch," Nick said, chuckling.

"No, I'm just kidding. My ex is dropping my son off tonight. It's my week. So, a teenage girl in my house with my teenage boy is a definite no go," Jones said.

Nick noticed that Anaya started drumming her fingers on the desktop uncomfortably at the mention of Jones's ex-wife. It was nothing overt. Her eyes closed just a fraction longer than a blink. The subtlety of the micro-gesture told a deeper story. Nick was intrigued but not sure he wanted the answer. Sometimes he felt it to be a curse that he was able to read people so well.

"I'm guessing that we're in agreement to keep this plan off the record?" Anaya asked.

"Absolutely. No boss is going to approve it," Nick said.

"Mouse, are you okay with this?" Anaya asked.

Mouse nodded.

"If anyone asks, I'm just going to say that CPS is handling her," Jones said.

"And I'll say that she is at APD headquarters for an interview," Anaya said.

"It sounds like we are a bunch of high schoolers planning to sneak out to a kegger," Nick said, laughing.

"Mouse, I'm going to need you to trust us. That means, you can't run away from us again. We can't protect you if we can't find you," Anaya said.

She leaned forward in the direction of the girl as she spoke and the movement loosened the shoulder strap of her blouse, exposing the light pink strap of her bra. The contrast in color to her dark brown skin was enthralling and Nick quickly averted his so as not to betray his sudden interest in the woman seated before him.

"Then it's settled. You two will look out for our little friend tonight and we'll reconvene in the morning," Jones said, grimacing as he looked down at his watch. "I have a standing order with the guys at headquarters that if any of the other girls start talking we are to be notified immediately. And Homicide will call if they catch a break."

They ambled out of the CPS office. Jones smiled and gave a two-fingered salute as he headed off in the direction of his car. Nick and Anaya stood silently and looked at each other for a moment before walking to his Jetta.

"We're going to need to grab some food on the way over to my place. It's a pretty sparse situation in my fridge right now," Nick said, embarrassed.

He was suddenly concerned about the impression his meager apartment would have on Anaya. *It's not like we're going on a date. But maybe that wouldn't be such a bad thing.* He pushed the thought from his head and refocused on the task ahead. Protecting Mouse from whoever was hunting her.

He started to doze off. The afternoon's sun had dipped behind the white concrete exterior of the Child Protective Services building. Cain's eyes no longer squinting against the brightness suddenly grew heavy. He'd trained himself to stay awake for days at a time. He prided himself on his control and was mad at himself for his momentary slip now. His neck cracked, releasing the tension built over the last several hours of sitting. The black Jetta that the Heathen had arrived in sat unmoved in the parking lot.

He adjusted the volume on the dashboard. The Pastor's words soothed:

If one is to walk without my hand, then he is alone. Alone to enter the darkness. Susceptible to its pull. Take hold. Allow my mighty grip to embrace your mortal fingers. Should you stumble then you will feel my strength. For in the darkness I never waver. My light burns eternal. Those that follow it will stay the path. And my path is the Way!

As if on cue, the front doors of the CPS headquarters opened. The Heathen exited, surrounded by the same three he'd seen earlier. *The friend of my enemy is my enemy.*

Chapter 28

The apartment's temperature was not much different than that of the outside. But after working up a light sweat from climbing the three flights of stairs to get its door, the ceiling fans running full speed did give a slight reprieve. Nick hustled in ahead of Anaya and Mouse. He cleared off the small round dining table adjacent to his living room and spread the food out. He tossed the stack of mail and magazines into a haphazard pile on the floor.

"Sorry, I wasn't expecting company," Nick said, apologetically.

"No need to explain. My place is pretty much the same. I spend more time in my office or car. I don't usually entertain guests either," Anaya said, giving a reassuring smile.

Nick returned the smile and walked into the living room. He pulled back the blinds and opened the sliding door. A light breeze cascaded in, granting additional relief. Hard to believe that it was only May and the heatwaves had already begun their assault. The word Spring held no meaning in Texas.

Mouse happily plopped in the seat with her back to the living room. She slid the padded straps free from her shoulders and laid the backpack down at her side. The weight of it a reminder of its deadly contents. The tall agent reached down to pick the bag up and her hand involuntarily snatched at it, pulling it away and further under her seat. He retracted his hand quickly and his eyes widened with a flash of shock.

"I didn't mean to startle you. I was just going to put your bag in the guest room," Nick said, diffusing the tension.

"Sorry," Mouse said, offering no further explanation.

She refused to release her grip of the bag's strap. She was convinced that the agent would feel the weight and know that something was off. It was a strange standoff and her heart fluttered with the anxiety of it.

Nick was looked down at the little girl, evaluating the obstinacy. He felt Anaya's hand on his right shoulder. The weight of it snapped him out of his bewilderment. Her fingers unknowingly caressed the scars where an enemy's rifle had long ago found its mark. He turned and faced her.

She stood close and he could smell something sweet in the air around her. Anaya glanced down at the backpack and gave a subtle shake of her head. Nick understood. Not worth battling with the girl over it. She's in a fragile state and it's probably become her security blanket.

"I've got a couple bottles of wine. Shiraz or Merlot?" Nick offered, breaking the tension.

He gestured over to the cheaply made wooden wine rack set atop his counter. The sparse selection of wine sat next to an overly-ripened banana that clung to the hanger from its blackened stem.

"I'm a sucker for either. You chose," Anaya said, batting her eyes slightly.

Anaya had a playfulness when she spoke with Nick that bordered on flirtatious. He liked it.

"Shiraz it is then. A favorite of my departed father," Nick said.

Nick reached into a cabinet above the rack and retrieved two stemmed wine glasses. He set them on the counter and began rummaging a drawer for the corkscrew.

"When did he pass?" Anaya said, catching the reference to his father's death.

"A couple years ago," Nick said.

"Sorry to hear that. I never really knew my parents. And what I do remember I'd rather forget," Anaya said, exposing herself.

She did not typically speak about her past and could not figure why she felt so inclined to do so with Nick.

"To pasts, good or bad, may they stay where they belong," Anaya said, redirecting the conversation away from personal landmines.

The clank of the wine glasses was louder than expected and Mouse looked up with a mouthful of cheeseburger. She looked more like a chipmunk than a mouse in her current feeding frenzy. She then went back to the food, grabbing a handful of fries. Nick and Anaya watched the small girl inhale the feast in front of her.

"You can shower or take a bath after dinner if you'd like?" Nick offered.

Mouse nodded. She leaned over her food. Her left arm a barrier between the two adults and the pile of French fries. Nick had seen inmates eat in a similar fashion. A primal need to protect their rations from the vultures.

"Take your time, hun. We're not in any rush. Eat, get cleaned up and, if you want, you can watch some television until you get tired," Nick said.

Mouse nodded again. She slowed her rate of consumption, but only slightly.

It was a nice apartment complex. The lighted pool looked inviting with its decorative fountain spitting water into the warm air of the evening. A couple sat closely in the hot tub, oblivious to the man in the Range Rover. The SUV was off, and the windows cracked slightly. He sat looking up toward the third-floor apartment. No binoculars were needed. Nor would they be prudent.

Cain took out his phone and confirmed the location. He reclined in the comfortable leather of the seats and then sent a text. *I should be done cleaning up in a little bit. Would you like to meet for a drink?*

The Pastor did not respond, but he knew that the messages were received, and its context would be understood. It was like talking to God. Like prayers whispered and with blind faith, believing that they were heard. He would wait. It was only a matter of time now.

"Why here?" Izzy asked.

The two friends gave a brief embrace and sat themselves in the black metal chairs of the pizza shop's street-side patio.

"Two reasons. One, I love it and, two, I can walk here," Declan said.

"Fair enough," Izzy said.

"Plus, Val and the girls are down the street at the creamery. They wanted to see you. I figured we could walk down and meet up with them after we had a chance to talk," Declan said.

"Sounds good. It's been too long. I'll bet the girls are growing fast," Izzy said.

She thought back to the first time she met his youngest, Laney. Not the kind of encounters that most people had. Trapped in a fully-engulfed mini-van.

The waiter quickly appeared and warmly greeted them. He smiled at Declan, recognizing him as a regular.

"We'll do a pitcher of Coors Light and a medium OMG," Declan said, without looking at the menu.

"OMG?" Izzy asked.

"It's not on the menu. A pizza covered in veggies and drizzled with a balsamic glaze. The call it the Oh My God pizza and only us regulars know about it," Declan said, winking.

The waiter nodded and took the menus, retreating into the restaurant.

"Sounds amazing," Izzy said.

"Trust me it is," Declan said. The smile faded and he continued, "Now back to the business at hand. Let's get this Nick thing sorted out."

"Well, as I said on the phone something is seriously wrong with him. Something's eating at him," Izzy said.

She cast her eyes downward and opened the napkin. She busied herself with the task of arranging the silverware.

"Agreed. My question is, how do we help him?" Declan asked.

"Not sure. I could call some friends in the bureau that I know out that way. Maybe they could lend a hand and check in on him," Izzy proposed.

"This is Nick we're talking about. He barely opened up to us. You can't ask a stranger to do it. He'd never bite," Declan said.

"Then what are you suggesting?" Izzy asked, cocking an eyebrow in suspicion of the former Frogman's thought process.

"Road trip," Declan said.

"Road trip?" Izzy retorted.

A cocky smile formed across his face, softening his rigid jawline.

Chapter 29

Nick and Anaya stood in the small kitchen leaning against the beige speckled counter. The two poured their second glass of wine while Nick cleaned up. Mouse finished her bath and was back in her clothes from earlier. She sat on the couch. Her wet hair flopped onto her shoulders. The dampness would be a welcome change. Even as darkness set, the heat of the day remained. Like a friend who refused to leave a party after its end.

"She seems to be doing well under the circumstances," Anaya whispered.

She moved close to Nick to relay the message so as not to disturb the girl's television-induced trance. Nick liked the way Anaya smelled. Her skin carried a hint of cherry or maybe plum. Whatever the fruit, it was sweet. Up close, he noticed that Anaya's eyes had flecks of amber and were dazzling. He looked away, immediately uncomfortable with his feelings.

Anaya remained close to him, standing still. She drew her lips into the slightest of smiles. So slight in fact, that Nick wasn't sure that his mind was playing tricks on him. As if taunting him further, she ran her finger slowly across the rim of the glass.

"She's as tough as they come," Nick said, breaking the tension.

"We need to get more out of her. Find out where she's from. If she's got family in the States," Anaya said, still whispering.

"We've also got to figure out who the assholes are that want this girl," Nick said, pausing only a moment before continuing, "Let's get her to bed. Maybe after a good night's sleep she'll be more apt to talk."

Anaya moved into the living room and leaned over the couch. Mouse was entranced by the television. She nodded absently at whatever the social worker had said, standing with a yawn. The two moved in tandem to the guest bedroom.

The room wasn't much more than four walls and a bed. Anaya tucked in the small girl and moved toward the door. As she clicked the light switch, Mouse mumbled a barely audible, "Thank you."

Anaya looked back, closing the door she said, "Get some rest, my brave little girl. You're safe now."

Nick had shut the TV off and the apartment took on a stillness. He met Anaya in the hallway as she exited the guest room.

"Sorry. Not much to the apartment. I haven't really done anything in the way of decorating since I moved in."

"Like I said before, no need to apologize. We're not so different." Anaya stretched. Her mind and body giving way to the stress of the day.

"You look beat. Take my bed. I've got the couch," Nick said.

"Don't be silly. This is your house. Sleep in your bed. Trust me, I'm no snob when it comes to comfort and your couch looks better than the cot in my office," Anaya chided, with a smile.

"I insist. I won't be able to fall asleep so quickly. If at all," Nick said.

He gave a slight bow and wave of his hand. His best attempt at a fairytale prince's curtsy. Anaya conceded to the agent's request and returned the bow, retreating to the back bedroom without further protest.

Nick grabbed a spare sheet from the hallway closet and tossed it on the end of the couch. It was warm now, but Texas temps in the Spring had a way of dipping low just before the dawn. In the quiet, he realized that he too was exhausted. He shut the living room light off The moon provided the room with a warm glow.

Nick sat on the couch. The soft, faux-leather exterior beckoned him to lay down. As his eyes fought the sleep that was fast approaching, his mind recalled the image of the dead girl and then of Mouse. *I'm not going to let that happen to you.* It was his last thought before he drifted off.

The lights in the apartment had gone off nearly an hour ago. Cain looked at his watch. It was only eleven. But it was Sunday. People did not typically stay up late with Monday's impending return to work. Yet he waited. He couldn't fail again. The Pastor would not be as forgiving a second time.

He listened. Over the last two hours, he'd acquainted himself with the complex. The couple in the hot tub left for their apartment, most likely to finish off the foreplay started beneath the bubbling water.

A security guard in an SUV, adorned with a yellow light on top, cruised through the lot twice. Each time it had been at the top of the hour. Routine lent to opportunity for men like Cain. The rent-a-cop had passed by a few minutes ago, meaning that he would not return for another hour. It didn't seem like he'd notice much anyway. On the two passes, the guard's head was looking down and the glow of his screen cast a white light on his face. Most likely consumed in the disconnected world of text messaging or social media.

He opened the door and stepped from the Range Rover. Cain's large frame expanded as he stretched. His size made the SUV look small in comparison. A yellow hue cast down from the light pole several feet away. The sweat on his bald head reflected a muted shine. He surveyed the lot one last time.

Satisfied that nobody was watching, he stepped off in the direction of the apartment building. Each step forward brought him closer to retrieving the Heathen. *Service its own reward.*

Chapter 30

The click startled her awake. It sounded louder in the silence of the night. Mouse never felt safe. No matter who was protecting her on the other side of that door. She remembered her dad's saying, *Sleep with one eye open*. She also remembered that she spent several days trying to accomplish that task. Mouse's father had laughed hard at his daughter's literal interpretation. She missed him. And she missed his lessons. But his skills were her skills now.

The backpack rested against the side of the bed and her left hand rummaged to the bottom, finding the butt of the gun. The metal felt cold and was an awkward fit for her small hands. It was a compact semi-automatic, which made it slightly easier to grip than a full-sized model. But the weapon's smaller frame wouldn't lessen the deadliness of it.

Big things come in small packages. Just like her.

For a large man, Cain moved with the soft steps of a cat. He allowed for his weight to transfer before taking each step, shifting heel to toe. After picking the apartment door's lock he entered, moving slowly across the tiled floor entranceway. Once he reached the living room area, he was able to step a little more quickly because of the carpet.

He didn't see him initially. This angered Cain. His sloppiness could have cost him the mission. He knew that he would need to press the blade in his pocket into his flesh to remove the sin. That would be later. He had work to do.

The man on the couch was sleeping. His feet hung over the far-side armrest. The heavy breathing indicated that he was not alerted to the man standing near. It would be quick and then he'd move on to the Heathen.

Cain slowly unsheathed a knife from the Kydex holster located in the small of his back and lowered himself, approaching the sleeping man's head on all fours. He displaced his body's girth among his four appendages, moving like a panther on the prowl.

Once in striking distance, Cain stopped. He listened. The man on the couch did not change the pattern of his rhythmic breathing.

He adjusted the tang of the double-sided blade in his right hand. The hilt of the black handle covered by his meaty thumb would be a counterbalance to the force as he drove the knife downward. *Pull the jaw toward him and drive deep.* Cain knew that to kill a man like this was not done with the gentle swipe of a blade. To kill a man by cutting his throat took strength. And it also took skill. It was important to execute the action without a sound to avoid alerting the others.

A friend of my enemy is my enemy! I am the Hand that delivers the truth!

Cain's left hand found its hold on the sleeping man's chin and he pulled back hard. The motion caused the man's neck to arch, exposing his throat. The knife came up high and the blade flashed in the moonlight. He drove down as a scream erupted in the hallway ahead of him, drawing his attention as his right arm continued to descend.

It wasn't a girly high-pitched scream. Mouse didn't make those. This was a warrior's release, like the men she'd read about in Colonel Chamberlain's ranks as they fixed bayonets and charged down Little Round Top in what became a turning point in the Battle of Gettysburg. She gave a battle cry! And it had the desired effect.

The large bald man looked at her for a split second. Momentarily caught off guard, but the knife was still moving. She pulled the trigger. The loud bang was deafening in the silence of the small apartment.

Shooting had always been an area of difficulty during her father's training. The adrenaline dump had made her hands moist with sweat. The recoil knocked the gun out of her two-handed grip. She didn't know if she'd hit the target. The muzzle flash in the darkness temporarily blinded her, losing sight of the dropped gun on the floor.

The knife struck down hard, but the scream and gunshot had redirected its aim. The sleeping man, who was no longer sleeping, grunted and spun away. The movement jerked the knife out of Cain's hand. His focus lost as a searing pain radiated from the left side of his neck. Involuntarily, he grabbed at it with his right hand. Like a reaction to a bee sting. His hand wet. He found the hole in his trapezius muscle near his neckline. Mentally, he triaged his wound. He'd live. His mind cleared, and he quickly turned his attention to the man on the ground.

The blade was still inside him. It was bad. *Who fired a shot? Where was his gun?* Nick's mind raced to comprehend the whirlwind of chaos that had just befallen him. It felt like a dream until the knife.

He saw the large man's bald head shimmer in muted light of the moon. He looked deranged. The left side of the man's off-white button-down shirt was covered in blood. The large bald man moved quickly. Faster than Nick.

The bald man's big fist struck hard into Nick's nose, just as he got himself to his knees. The blow landed with a dizzying effect. Nick was on all fours now, flickering in and out of consciousness. He shook his head, trying to clear his head and get himself into the fight. A hard impact across the back of Nick's neck sent him face-down into the carpet, burying the knife deeper into his side. The pain kept him from blacking out, but only barely.

A blur of movement shot by the couch, nearly eclipsed by the bald man's frame. The large man straddled him, and the impressive weight forced the air out of his lungs. The pressure of the man's grip was unbearable. Nick clawed at the fingers that were coiled around his throat, squeezing relentlessly. His energy to fight left him as the blood poured from his wound. Made worse from the lack of oxygen created by his neck's constriction. Several loud bangs rang out as Nick's vision failed and he slipped into darkness.

Chapter 31

"When you make a decision to do something there is no hesitation, huh?" Izzy said, rhetorically.

"Kind of my thing. My wife has a love-hate relationship with it. Saves the hemming and hawing, but sometimes the quick decision leaves us spinning," Declan said, accelerating the rental car, a white Camry, around the commuters in the middle lane.

Declan thought back about his decision with the bank. In hindsight, he wished he'd come up with a better alternative. It was hard to put himself back into that desperate state of mind now that he'd come out of their financial slump. At the time, it seemed hopeless. He had long since surrendered to the guilt of his conscience. And he hoped that he came up with an acceptable way of atoning.

"If you keep driving like this then we'll make great time," Izzy said, peering at the speedometer.

They'd been driving for a few hours and had already crossed over the border of Connecticut.

"We're going to drive straight through. So, you might want to get some rest now. I'm going to be tapping you in before you know it," Declan said, smiling.

"I know he sounded like he needed us, but what's the urgency?" Izzy asked.

"That gut feeling. I can't quite place it, but whatever he's dealing with I figure the sooner we get the better off he'll be," Declan said.

"I learned to trust your gut instinct," Izzy said, chuckling.

She thought back to Declan's uncanny ability to get a handle on the terrorist attacks last Fall. Then she added, "It feels strange to be making a trip like this again."

"I'm glad you said that. The hairs on the back of my neck have been standing on end since we left," Declan said.

Expelling the words caused his shoulders to slump. A burden lifted.

Izzy pulled the lever on side of her seat and reclined. She stretched and turned to her side, exposing a tribal tattoo on her lower back. Declan caught a glimpse of the artwork and smiled. He knew Izzy well enough to know that she had a wild side, but seeing the ink removed any trace of doubt.

Lane markers zipped by as he refocused his eyes to the road ahead and settled into the drive. For some reason, he felt that the clock was ticking, but to what end he had no idea.

Chapter 32

The air had cooled. No humidity lingered. Even with those two factors Mouse was drenched in sweat. She'd been alternating between running and walking for the last hour or so. She saw a lighted display under a bank sign. *1:07 am and 62 degrees.*

Mouse stopped, figuring that she'd created enough distance from the apartment where the bald man had come for her. She reached into her backpack, now slightly lighter without the gun, and pulled out a plastic water bottle. She sipped, controlling her desire to guzzle the tepid water. She needed to conserve it until she got to her destination. The problem was she didn't have a clue as to where she was.

She saw a sign for the interstate and moved in that direction. She skirted along side streets to avoid the bald man or anyone else that may be looking for her. A girl walking alone at night might draw attention. But the streets were deserted for the most part.

The bright yellow from the Shell Gas Station's illuminated seashell caught her attention and she crossed West University Avenue, heading for the store. There were a few cars parked in front and one at the pumps. Mouse passed by and entered into the air-conditioning of the store. It was funny to see the woman behind the register wearing a sweater, but it was definitely cold inside. The little girl's arms prickled with goosebumps as she navigated the aisles. She took the opportunity to stock up for the next leg of her journey, grabbing Gatorade and beef jerky.

She walked to the counter and sized up the large Hispanic woman at the register. Mouse debated on speaking in Spanish but didn't. She thought that English would make her seem American and draw less suspicion.

"Well hello, little one," the clerk said.

She had no hint of an accent, confirming that English would be the best choice for this conversation.

"Hi there," Mouse replied, in a diminutive manner.

"You're out late tonight," the large woman said.

"I know. I messed up. I got in a fight with my mom," Mouse said, looking down and away. She wanted to give the impression of a troubled teenager.

"How bad?" the clerk asked.

"It's my fault. I said some really mean things and then I ran away," Mouse said, keeping up her act. She continued before the woman could speak, "I just want to go back home, but I don't have a ride. Would you be able to call me a cab?"

"I could, but maybe it's better that I call the police," the woman said.

She didn't say this in a threatening manner. More so in the form of a question. As if she were asking the girl for her opinion or permission.

"Please don't! That will only make it worse." Mouse turned on the waterworks and sobbed, generating tears for effect.

"Don't cry, little one," the large clerk said.

It was working. The woman had bought the act.

"Please," Mouse pleaded, softly.

"Okay. Where do you live?" the woman asked. Mouse looked at her with distrust and the woman registered this and responded, "It's not for the police. It's for the cab company. They will need to know where they're driving to."

"Austin. Downtown area," Mouse said, casting her eyes downward again.

"Well you did make it pretty far in your journey tonight," the woman said, sounding impressed.

"Where am I?" Mouse asked, gathering the info in the hopes that she could get a newspaper tomorrow and would open it to find an article about a dead bald man in an apartment shooting.

"You're in Georgetown. About fifteen miles north of Austin. Let me see what I can do for you," the woman said, sweetly.

"Thank you," Mouse replied.

"How about an Uber? They are usually quicker than any cab company these days," the woman said, smiling.

"What's an Uber?" Mouse asked. It was a funny word and she'd never heard of it before.

"It's like a cab, but people use their own cars. Don't worry, it's safe," The woman said and then continued, "I use it all the time. Tell you what. I will get you an Uber. I'll put in my account. You save your money."

"That's very kind of you," Mouse said.

The woman punched at the screen on her phone and then said, "See, how easy is that?"

The woman turned the screen toward Mouse and she watched as the computerized map showed a car icon moving toward a blue dot.

"That's us. And that's your driver. He'll be here in less than three minutes. Pretty cool, huh?" The woman was proud of this technology.

"Very cool," Mouse said.

Happy to be getting out of the city with the bald man. She'd heard the additional gunshots as she fled through the parking lot and hoped that he was now a dead bald man.

But if there was one thing Mouse's fifteen years of life had taught her, it was that hopes and wishes are the things of fairy tales.

Chapter 33

It was overcast, but the morning's light seemed bright as it passed through the windshield, pulling Izzy from her sleep. Her neck was sore from the awkward position she'd taken during the night. She looked at the clock. 6:43 am. Then she looked over at Declan. His eyes were focused on the road but she could tell that he was struggling against exhaustion. His shoulders were hunched forward and he was holding onto the steering wheel as if he was drowning and it was a life preserver.

"Why didn't you wake me?" Izzy asked, wiping the sleep from her eyes.

"I got my second wind in the middle of the night. I figured I'd push on and let you rest. You can take over at the next exit I see with a gas station. We need to fill up anyway," Declan said. Fatigue gave his words a slight slur.

"I need a cup of coffee to get my blood pumping," Izzy said with a yawn, bringing the seat into an upright position. "How long have you been awake?"

"Not counting the power nap I took before I picked you up?" Declan asked, but continued before allowing for the answer, "Roughly twenty-eight hours."

"Holy crap! You must be seeing double," Izzy said.

"Nah, that was hours ago. I'm seeing triple now," Declan laughed.

"I'm going to reach out to Nick before I take over the drive. I think it's best we don't surprise him," Izzy said.

"Okay. Maybe just feel him out a bit before you tell him we're on our way. I don't want him to flip out before we get a chance to have a face-to-face with him," Declan said.

The phone rang twice and then clicked. The cellular acknowledgment that the call had connected.

"Hello," the voice on the other end said.

"Who's this?" Izzy asked. Her tone was a blend of confusion and anger at hearing a female's voice on the other end of Nick's line.

"I apologize. I'm Anaya, a friend of Nick's," Anaya said, calmly.

"Where's Nick?" Izzy asked. The sudden wave of jealousy that overcame Izzy forbid her from being any less direct.

"He's right here," Anaya said softly and then continued, "He's..."

"Well, put him on the phone," Izzy interrupted.

"I can't. He's unconscious," Anaya said, sounding standoffish.

"What do you mean unconscious?" Izzy asked.

"Who may I ask is calling?" Anaya asked. Her voice strengthened in tone.

"Izzy Martinez, FBI," Izzy said, curtly.

"Oh, I'm sorry, Agent Martinez. I didn't know that you were with the Bureau," Anaya said, see-sawing back to a softer inflection.

"Tell me what's going on with Nick." Izzy did not bother to minimize her official title for this woman. For some reason, she liked that Anaya had felt the need to address her as Agent.

"We were attacked last night. Nick took the worst of it. He came out of surgery about an hour ago, but he hasn't woken yet. The doctor was just in and said that Nick's in stable condition," Anaya said, giving a very brief summary of the events leading up to this hospital visit.

"Attacked? By whom? Surgery? I need details!" Izzy said, angrily.

She was angered at hearing that Nick was injured, but more so that some random woman was by his side instead of her.

"We were protecting a young victim. Well, correction, Nick was doing the protecting. I'm the CPS caseworker assigned to the girl. Anyway, Nick decided that the girl would be safer at his place," Anaya said.

"What? Nick brought a victim to his home?" Izzy interrupted. The frustration evident in her voice.

"Yes. I know that it's not normal procedure, but this is not a typical situation," Anaya said.

"Go on," Izzy prodded.

"A man came for the girl during the night. Nick was stabbed and beaten," Anaya said. Her voice trembled as she retold the violent encounter.

"Stabbed? How bad?" Izzy asked, dropping the jealous frustration from her voice. A genuine concern for Nick was the only thing that could be heard in the questions.

"The knife wound was just above the left hip. It's bad. I thought he was dead. There was so much blood," Anaya mumbled the last part, trailing off in thought.

"Jesus," Izzy whispered.

Declan looked at his friend in the passenger seat. Izzy, who'd proven that she was as tough as any operator he'd worked with, looked shaken. The color drained from the dark olive skin. He was able to gather from the one side of the conversation that things were worse than they'd thought. Subconsciously, he pressed the gas pedal, urging the Camry forward.

"The doctor said that he was lucky. He said that the blade missed the kidney, but it went deep. Thankfully, it didn't exit out the back. The doctor said that might've been much worse. Something about it being much easier to pack a wound with one hole," Anaya said, pausing as she staved off the wooziness created by the recall of the wound.

She been the one to press the dishrags hard against Nick's side. The memory of their wetness sickened her. The stains on her unchanged clothes a reminder to the volume of blood spilled.

"Are you going to stay with him?" Izzy asked.

"Yes. Unless they find the girl. Then I'd have to help on that end," Anaya said.

"We're on our way. Just coming up on Knoxville. We should be there by ten tonight," Izzy said, looking at Declan for confirmation of the timeline.

He nodded in response without taking his eyes off the road.

"I'll call you back at this number if something changes," Anaya said.

"Thank you," Izzy said. She then added, "What happened to the asshole that stabbed Nick?"

"I shot at him and he ran away," Anaya said.

"Shot at him? Did you hit him?" Izzy asked. She realized that her tone more accusatory than intended but didn't apologize for it.

"I'm not sure. I've never fired a gun before. I pulled the trigger until it was empty. He ran out the door. There was so much blood. I'm not sure if it was from him or Nick," Anaya said, trying to explain herself to the agent.

"Regardless, it sounds like if you hadn't been there then Nick would be dead," Izzy said.

"I really don't want to think about it," Anaya said, reflecting back to the lighthearted moment drinking wine with Nick in the kitchen.

"Who is he working with on this, besides you?" Izzy asked.

"Detective Jones from APD," Anaya said.

"Send his contact info to me," Izzy requested.

"I will. He's out looking for the girl as we speak," Anaya said.

"She's gone?" Izzy asked.

"Yes."

Anaya did not add anything more. The implication of the girl being outside of the protection of law enforcement didn't bode well for her survival. And the thought of it saddened her deeply.

"Keep me posted. If he wakes up, tell him that I'm on my way and that Declan is with me," Izzy said.

She clicked the end button and the image of Nick's chat head disappeared from her screen. She closed her eyes and released this new-found tension, exhaling slowly.

"That didn't sound good," Declan said, stating the obvious.

"Well, you couldn't have been more right," Izzy said, pausing for effect before she continued, "Nick needs our help."

The hum of the vent and vibrations of the Greyhound bus lulled Mouse to sleep. Her eyes would pop open anytime it slowed or stopped. She would scan for threats and then fade out. The bus was approaching Dallas, where she would switch to another bus. The itinerary acquired for her by the homeless man showed that there would be a total of four transfers until she reached the bus's final destination of Saginaw, Michigan.

It was not restful sleep but, with every rotation of the wheels, she was farther away from the men who hunted her. Sitting in the back of the bus allowed for her to see the scattered heads of the other passengers. Mouse folded her backpack into a pillow and positioned it between her and the bus's frame.

She closed her eyes and tried to envision what Lake Huron would look like. The starting point for her new life.

Chapter 34

Pain was not a new sensation and its presence now was not unwelcomed. He'd long ago severed the emotional connection with it. He was aware of his damaged body but was able to compartmentalize. Evaluating his injuries, Cain slid his right hand from one to the next. The hole near his neck was still a concern, but he also had located two more places where he was struck during the second burst of gunfire.

The outer portion of his left thigh had been hit and Cain took a grazing shot to his left bicep. The flesh wound on his arm didn't even register as a concern to him. It could be repaired with a few stitches or left to heal on its own and serve as a reminder of his second failed attempt. He felt around the circumference of his meaty thigh and was unable to locate an exit wound. That could be problematic. Retrieval of the lodged round could cause some additional damage.

The bleeding coming from his arm and neck had slowed with the applied pressure. The Quick Clot that he'd poured on it also played a part. His survival bag was equipped to handle some potential trauma, but it only would serve as a temporary fix until he could get medical attention. In his line of work, going to a conventional hospital would be unacceptable. Too many questions. Answers to which would land him in jail for the rest of his life.

After fleeing the apartment complex, he had driven until he found a dive-bar outside of the city and had stopped there to triage his wounds. He had figured that he'd be less likely to be noticed by the drunken patrons meandering into the watering hole. Once Cain stabilized his injuries, he wiped his hands on his pants to remove the wet blood and then pulled out his phone. He wanted nothing more than to push on and find the Heathen, but he knew that, if he wasn't patched up properly, he wouldn't be physically capable of carrying out the task. He made the call.

A frail man with wisps of gray in his hair that stood over him wore a faded white medical coat. No name tag. No hospital. He didn't speak and Cain was glad because he was in no mood to engage in small talk. This doctor knew not to ask questions and was paid well for his discretion. In times past, men like this had assisted in mending his damaged body. The consequences of his service to the Pastor. His service as God's Hand.

As he lay on the improvised operating table in the empty warehouse waiting for the surgeon to begin his work, he recalled the phone conversation with the Pastor.

"Where are you, my son?" the Pastor said.

His words were similar to that of a concerned parent.

"I failed you," Cain uttered.

"Failure is another opportunity to prove yourself, my son," the Pastor said. It was something he'd often repeated during his sermons.

Another opportunity to serve, Cain thought.

A tear rolled down his cheek as the surgeon began digging into his leg to retrieve the bullet. The tear was not out of pain, but joy. An overwhelming sense of happiness filled him at the thought of his redemption.

Chapter 35

Rusty stood in the parking lot of the Shell gas station, sweating profusely from the recent track. A bowl of Evian water was being lapped at loudly by his partner. The track had taken the pair from the Water's Edge Apartment complex along the San Gabriel River and came to an end at the entrance to the mini-mart of the gas station. Several members of the Georgetown Police Department were on scene and had assisted. Jones was inside talking with the clerk, a heavy-set Hispanic woman. He exited a short time later as Jasper retreated to the backseat of the Crown Vic to lay down.

"Damn do-gooder!" Jones huffed.

"What's up?" Rusty asked, trying to get a read on the detective's comment.

"She got the kid a ride. She actually Ubered her back to Austin!" Jones seethed. He made no effort to hide the frustration of this added complication.

"Shit!" Rusty said.

He too had become emotionally invested in this case and, in particular, finding this missing girl. He was concerned that the next track would lead him to another small, lifeless body. The thought caused the seasoned tracker to shiver involuntarily.

"The Uber app on her phone showed the location where she was dropped off, but we are way behind the power curve on finding her." Jones said.

The pudgy detective looked at his watch as he spoke and nervously rubbed at his temple. The track hadn't been run until Nick was transported and the crime scene was worked. Georgetown's detective division was still processing the apartment. Crucial time had been lost in the chaos.

Anaya had called Jones and notified him. He'd responded quickly, but with every passing minute the likelihood of finding the girl dissipated. Austin and Georgetown PD had an excellent working relationship and Jones filled in their investigators on the case up to this point when he arrived on scene.

"It's already past eight. The Uber dropped her off a few hours ago at the same damn Holiday Inn on Middle Fiskville Road that we found her at last time. Why there?" Jones paused as his brain struggled to make the connection.

"Beats me but we should get Jasper over that way and see what we can find," Rusty said.

"We better figure it out before someone else does," Jones said. There was an ominous tone in his statement.

"Any word on the guy who attacked them?" Rusty asked.

"There's footage of a Range Rover exiting around the timeline established. The Georgetown guys are working on trying to get a plate and an image of our guy. Nothing yet," Jones said.

"I'm here for whatever you need on this," Rusty said, looking back at the Crown Vic that contained his painting partner.

"With Nick out of commission and the girl on the run, I'm gonna need you two more than ever," Jones replied, slipping back into his Texas drawl for effect.

Jones spoke briefly to the sergeant on scene at the gas station before departing for Austin with Rusty and his four-legged partner following close behind in their cruiser. He hoped that they would have as easy a time of locating her at the hotel as they did before.

Chapter 36

"How's he doing?" Jones asked, holding the phone to his ear as he drove.

"He's still out. Hopefully, he'll wake soon. He's stirred a few times but hasn't opened his eyes yet." Anaya relayed this in her gentle tone. She then added, "Any luck on your end?"

"Dead end. We checked the hotel. No sign of her. Nothing on camera. Jasper didn't locate a track," Jones said, sounding disheartened.

"Damn. That's a problem. Any ideas?" Anaya asked.

"We're heading back to headquarters. I've got to push one of the girls from the hotel to give us something. Otherwise, we're running blind," Jones said.

"I'll meet you there. Maybe I can help you with coaxing some info out of them. I'm not doing much here. The FBI assigned a two-agent protective detail for his room. They said they'll let us know if Nick wakes," Anaya said.

"We'll see you there," Jones said, ending the call as he merged into traffic.

The girls saved from the depravity of the Stagecoach Inn had eaten and slept. Jones's unit had a room with two beds. It was typically used for the detectives when a major case dictated long hours, but it also served its purpose in situations like this as well. They had to add three cots to accommodate the five girls.

When Anaya clicked the light, it looked more like a sleepover party. All five girls were snuggled into the two twin beds. It made sense; they were scared. She understood the unbreakable bond they shared. Connected through dire circumstance.

"Good morning, girls," Anaya announced, softly. She did not want to startle them.

Murmured grunts and groans floated across the room as the girls adjusted to the introduction of light. Slowly, one by one, they sat up, rubbing their eyes and yawning. They looked inquisitively at the woman standing in the doorway.

Anaya didn't speak Spanish. Although, in her many years of working in Austin she'd seen the need and vowed to one day learn it. She'd planned to do a lot of things, but life seemed to get in the way. She could fill this small room with her *to do* list.

A translator from the detective unit stood behind her as she spoke, translating verbatim. "Girls, I need your help. Another girl is in trouble. The same people that did this to you are after her. We need to find her before they do," Anaya said, waiting as the message was relayed to them in their native tongue.

Most of the girls stared vacantly at the social worker. Not in defiance. More in an indifference. The brutality of their past circumstance depleted their empathy. Anaya knew this because she'd gone through it herself. Some victims never regained their sense of self.

One girl, a thirteen-year-old who referred to herself as Maria during intake, nodded slightly at the request. It was a subtle gesture, but Anaya was relieved to see it.

"Come with me," Anaya said, gesturing with her hand as if beckoning a toddler to walk.

Maria looked around at her bunkmates timidly, hesitating momentarily as she slipped off the bed. She walked to the doorway and didn't look back at the other girls, not wanting to see the judgment in their eyes. Anaya received her with a smile and escorted her out of the room. The remaining four girls resumed their supine positions as the light clicked off and the door closed.

Maria sat on a couch and Anaya in a chair positioned adjacent to her. The room had pale pink walls with three framed paintings, each depicting sunsets in swirl of bright colors. Potted plants were set in the two far corners. Out of context, it would look more like a small living room. It was done so by design. A room created to facilitate communication from young victims. Sad that such a room was needed. Sadder that it was needed with such an increased frequency.

Jones watched on the other side through the one-way mirror. Unlike the portrayal of television's numerous police dramas, investigators did not typically interview child victims. That was handled by a select group of trained social workers. These forensic interviews were designed to elicit conversations without any manipulation, using a nationally recognized set of protocols. Anaya was qualified to conduct the interview. Something that she excelled at it. The translator sat in a folding chair positioned directly behind Maria to ensure that the girl would only look and speak toward the interviewer.

The flow was slow at first, with the delay of each question being converted for Maria. The translator also relayed Maria's responses in English for Anaya. But beyond the technical aspect of the interview's pace, it was further hampered by Maria's resistance to talk about her situation. Typical of these victims, but with the clock ticking on Mouse it was more frustrating than usual. Anaya fought hard to suppress her anxiety.

"Maria, we need to find her. Her life depends on it," Anaya said, almost pleading with the teen.

Anaya sat drumming her fingers against her notepad as the words were translated. At the conclusion of the translation, Maria's head dipped a fragment lower in a mannerism that could only be described as sad.

Then Maria spoke for the first time since entering the room. She whispered, "They will find her. They always do."

The words, spoken in English, caught both Anaya and the translator by surprise. Anaya didn't admonish the child for holding back. She understood it. She knew that it was the girl's last defensive weapon and that she had just lowered her imaginary sword of distrust.

"What do you mean *they always do*?" Anaya asked.

"I got away once. Not for long, but I did," Maria said, a small swell of pride entering her diminutive voice.

"What happened?" Anaya asked.

"I was small back then. I got out through a bathroom window at one of the motels," Maria said, pausing for approval before she continued, "I thought that I had escaped." The teenager's voice trailed off at this last statement.

"How long did it take for them to find you?" Anaya asked.

"Not long," Maria said, flatly.

"What happened then?" Anaya asked, afraid of the child's answer.

Maria didn't answer. The emotional wall took shape again. The girl's eyes look distant.

"How did they find you?" Anaya asked, redirecting the dialogue back to her comfort zone.

Maria shrugged. "They shouldn't have. I was hiding in a tunnel pretty far away from the motel," Maria said, looking for the social worker to provide an insight.

"Did they see you run off?" Anaya asked.

"I don't think so. I was hiding and a man appeared out of nowhere. He told me to come with him. He had a gun, so I listened," Maria said, defensively.

"And then what happened?"

"He took me somewhere else," Maria whispered. Her strength zapped.

The teenager pulled her knees to her chest and wrapped her arms tightly around them. She began a gentle rocking motion. The trauma of that memory was still raw. Anaya assumed that this was probably the first time that she'd spoken about it to anyone.

"You're very brave, Maria. I hope you know that. I hope you understand how special you really are," Anaya said.

The words were designed to soothe the girl after this retelling. But they couldn't have been truer. Some people repressed the memories of such trauma so deeply that the words to describe it are lost forever.

"What happens to us now?" Maria asked, softly.

"I will make sure that you're safe. Those people will not hurt you ever again!" Anaya said, with conviction in her voice.

"They'll find me again," Maria said, with a shiver.

"I promise you that will not happen," Anaya said, but the confidence backing that statement waned. Especially, after the recent events with Mouse.

"I'm tired," Maria said.

Anaya registered the girl's comment and understood its meaning. She was done talking and Anaya knew better than to push any further.

"Thank you for speaking with me, Maria. You were very helpful."

Anaya escorted the girl back to the room. Maria quietly scampered back into the bed and found a comfortable spot among the sprawled bodies. She was quickly swallowed up by the scattered blankets and into the arms of friends. Her safety net.

"Well, what do you think?" Jones asked as Anaya returned.

The two now stood in the disarray of Jones's cubicle looking at each other. Anaya drummed her fingers and Jones rubbed his stomach.

"At least she's talking. That's a huge first step in the right direction for us," Anaya said, optimistically.

"True, but time isn't on our side. We don't have the luxury of waiting around to slowly bleed information out of these girls," Jones said.

Frustration had set in and the comment's tone came out rougher than intended. Jones quickly fumbled to add, "Sorry. I'm worried about the girl and I'm pissed off at what happened to Nick. I want this guy bad. I want his whole damn crew!"

"Me too," Anaya said, placing her hand on his shoulder.

The touch's effect was immediate. It did two things simultaneously. It calmed him, but also excited him. Jones regretted that his cheeks coloring did little to hide his emotions. He nodded and looked away, pretending to look for something in his stack of files.

"Next step?" Anaya asked.

"I've got every cop in the city keeping an eye out for the girl. The traffic unit is checking intersection cameras and license-plate readers to see if we can get a plate on the Range Rover. Maybe something will break in our favor," Jones said.

He'd deployed similar tactics on abduction cases in the past and sometimes these measures helped. Sometimes it was the simplest of things that broke a case wide open. The infamous Son of Sam serial killer, David Berkowitz, was eventually caught because of a parking ticket.

"Who knows, maybe we'll get a sighting of her and Rusty can track her down again," Anaya said, widening her eyes with a hopeful look.

Anaya rubbed her head. With the short interview completed and a lull in pace since the tumultuous events of the night, she was suddenly overwhelmed by exhaustion. She yawned as if trying to swallow all the air from the building.

"Get some rest. Rusty is refueling his vehicle and his partner. I've got it for a few hours while you reset yourself," Jones said, giving a half-smile.

He attempted to give Anaya a comforting pat on her shoulder, but as he turned the wide girth of his midriff tapped a teetering stack of papers. It was like pulling the wrong Jenga piece. A tidal wave of file folders splashed to the floor.

Jones reddened with a combination of embarrassment and exertion as he bent down. Suddenly, he stopped his feverish attempt at reorganization. He stood holding several 8x10 glossies. His eyes were transfixed on the images.

"What's up?" Anaya asked, noticing that Jones was lost deep in thought.

"Not sure," Jones mumbled, still staring at the pictures.

Anaya circled behind the detective and stood on her tippy toes to look over his shoulder at the images.

The two stared at the closeup images of the motel room girls' burned hiplines. Jones shuffled between the branding mark of the eleven-year-old and the others. The doctor said that the eleven-year-old's burn had been done recently. He stated that pinkness and irritation of skin indicated that it was still healing. Something caught the eye of the seasoned detective when he compared this girl's picture to the others.

"Why does that one look different?" Anaya asked.

She was so close to him that her voice startled him. Feeling her warm breath on his neck momentarily derailed his train of thought. He quickly regained his composure and cleared his throat.

"Not sure, but it almost looks like there's a square underneath it. Like something under the skin is framing the burn."

"Okay?" Anaya said in a questioning tone.

She was still confused at the observation. Angry at herself for not being able to see what he was getting at.

"I want to get these girls back to the hospital. Now! I know that I just told you to go home and get some rest, but I could really use your help with this," Jones said, his eyes pleading.

"You don't even have to ask. There's no way I'd be able to fall asleep anyway. At least not until we find Mouse and I know that Nick's going to be okay," Anaya said.

"I'm going to let my boss know that we're going to be taking them back to medical." Jones said.

He was already moving. He headed in the direction of his boss's corner office with the file folder containing the images loosely tucked under his arm.

"I'll start rousing the girls," Anaya said, heading back toward the room where she'd just brought Maria.

Anaya quietly turned the knob and opened the door. She allowed the light to spill in from the office area and fill the room. Maria sat upright first. She cocked her head and raised one eyebrow. The question on her face was obvious. *What do you want now?*

"We need to go back to the hospital. Can you tell the others?" Anaya asked in a whisper.

She knew the importance of empowering the teenager by giving her a role. It would be much more agreeable to the other girls if the request came from Maria. By default, she'd become their leader and they'd trust her over any cop or social worker.

Maria nodded and began whispering to the other girls crammed on the beds. Anaya was glad to see Maria's willingness to help. It would be beneficial to the investigation. But, more importantly, it gave Anaya hope that the girl would be strong enough to later battle the demons of her recent past.

Chapter 37

The fluorescent light bled into his eyes, causing them to water. With each blink, his surroundings became clearer. He looked at the intravenous line running from the back of his hand up to the clear plastic bag hanging off the thin metal rack. Nobody was in the room, but he could hear voices outside. The blinds were drawn and the analog clock on the wall said 8:52. Nick had no idea if it was morning or night. The disoriented confusion bothered him.

He adjusted himself in the bed when he heard the click of the door's latch. His left side protested the movement. The pain was strong enough to make him wince. Nick was prepared for a more intense sensation and the dull throb indicated that he was on pain meds. The fog in his head was also a telling sign.

"Mr. Lawrence, I'm glad to see that you're awake." The nurse said as she entered the room.

She approached slowly, first checking several of the machines surround his bed. She picked up his hand that had the IV attached and manipulated it checking the tape. She placed his hand back on the bed without much care.

"What's the damage?" Nick mumbled. His speech was impacted by the dryness of his mouth.

"The doctor will be in shortly to go over everything with you. How are you feeling?" She asked, with a curtness that was neither rude nor pleasant.

"I feel like someone stabbed me," Nick said, making a feeble attempt at levity.

"Very funny, Mr. Lawrence. On a scale of one to ten, how would you rate your discomfort?" the nurse asked, dryly.

"I feel good. The pain isn't bad at all. I would give it a three," Nick said, hoping that his self-evaluation would lead to a speedy discharge. He hated hospitals and wanted to leave as soon as he was able.

"Well, you're a very tough man. Most people wouldn't be so lighthearted after going through an ordeal like yours." The nurse gave a flaccid smile.

"I've been through worse." Nick paused, recalling the injuries sustained from the standoff with the Translator eight months ago. The reminders of those wounds still plagued him. He continued, "How long until I'm out of here?"

"Let's not put the cart before the horse. You've got quite a bit of recovery time before you're going to be out chasing bad guys," the nurse said, sounding like a parent trying to get her child to eat his vegetables.

Nick didn't respond. He would save his argument about an early discharge for the doctor. The nurse set about her business, re-checking the different monitors and notating the information on a chart.

"Are you up for some company while you wait for the doctor?" the nurse asked, as she made her way to the door.

"Sure," Nick said, softly.

"Well, this damn case went to hell in a handbasket quicker than shit," Jones said, as he strolled into the room with Anaya in tow.

Jones's drawl was in full effect. He even added a slight swagger to his walk. Nick watched the Austin detective saunter to his bedside, imagining him in a pair of spurs and a ten-gallon hat. Nick laughed to himself at the thought.

"Hey Jones, don't get all emotional on my account. I don't want you to drown yourself in stress-induced brisket-eating-frenzy on my account," Nick retorted, sarcastically.

"This is what you need, my fit friend," Jones said, gripping the excess around his waistline. Chuckling, he added, "Extra bulletproofing! I'll bet that knife wouldn't've even penetrated my outer layer"

"How are you feeling?" Anaya said, not giving into the childish banter of the two investigators.

"I'm good as gold," Nick said, repositioning himself to look at Anaya.

"I answered your phone for you while you were out of it." Anaya said, sheepishly.

Her fingers twiddled, and she dropped her eyes slightly. Anaya had a worried look, as though she was a child admitting to stealing a candy bar.

"Thanks. Anything important?" Nick asked, showing that he wasn't fazed at all by the intrusion.

"It was a friend of yours," Anaya said, pausing for a moment before she continued. "Izzy."

Nick saw the slightest of facial tics in Anaya's face at the mention of Izzy. Her left cheek muscle spasmed, pulsing once. Nick knew that it was an involuntary response. He wasn't sure of its meaning but was intrigued by the prospects.

"Oh, what did she say?" Nick asked, hoping to see another reaction.

"She said to tell you that she was on her way. She also told me to tell you that Declan was with her," Ayana said, relaying the message. This time without the tic.

"What? Why?" Nick asked. The question was more to himself, knowing that Anaya wouldn't hold the answer.

Anaya shrugged.

"I've got something big!" Jones said, slapping a manila folder on the railing of the hospital bed.

Nick waited, knowing that Jones was only pausing for effect and would give the big reveal to his news without further prompting.

"Check this out," Jones said, opening the file and sliding out a photograph.

Jones handed over the glossy image. Nick held it close to his face. His eyes scanned the image. He'd already seen it before and squinted hard, wondering what detail he missed.

"Maybe I'm still coming off the anesthesia but isn't that the same picture I already saw?" Nick said, confused.

Jones smiled, frustrating him further. He was going to make him work for it. Nick again looked at the image of a branded hip of one of the girls from the motel.

"It is, but we missed something the first time around. Look carefully," Jones said, teetering on the verge of giddy.

Nick cocked his eyebrow, showing his disinterest in playing this game any further with his Austin counterpart.

"I give up. What am I looking at?" Nick asked, sighing loudly.

"I didn't see it at first either. None of us did," Jones said.

The portly detective leaned over the railing of Nick's hospital bed. His belly pressed hard against it, spilling over onto Nick's arm as he pointed at the squared outline that framed the brand. He retracted and shoved his hand into his pants pocket.

"Look at this," Jones said, holding up a plastic bag.

"What's that?" Nick asked, looking at the small black objects inside. They were the size and shape of scrabble tiles.

"I've never seen anything like this before. Have you?" Jones asked.

Jones raised both eyebrows expressively as his eyes widened. He tossed the bag to Nick. It landed on his chest. The contents of the ziplock jingled.

Nick clicked the button on the bed, bringing him into a more upright position. The excitement about this new bit of evidence muted out the pain of the movement. He held the bag in his hand and delicately manipulated its contents.

"Is this what I think it is?" Nick asked, almost gasping.

"Your guess is as good as mine, but I'm gonna go out on a limb and say that we're looking at some type of computer chip," Jones replied.

"Holy shit! That explains a lot," Nick said.

The realization came crashing down on him. He quickly surmised that this is how the bald man found the girl at his apartment, shaking his head in disbelief.

"I've heard of trafficking organizations using things like this to keep tabs on their merchandise but have never seen it in person," Anaya said, inserting herself into the conversation.

"They track them. Makes sense. This is big business and they appear to have come up with a way to control their assets," Nick said.

"This group has got to be big time. A low-level operation isn't going to have the funds to support this kind of technology," Jones said. He added, "I'm going to get these over to digital and see what they can come up with."

"Leave one with me. I want to run it by someone," Nick said.

Nick saw Jones grimace at this request. Without waiting for approval, he opened the bag and slipped his fingers in, retrieving one of the black chips.

"If this is some type of tracking device then we have a much bigger problem," Anaya said, pausing momentarily before she continued, "Mouse. There is no place that she can run that they won't be able to find her."

"That's why we've got to find her first," Nick said.

"What's this we stuff. You were turned into a human pincushion a few hours ago. You're not going anywhere,"

Jones said, looking down at Nick's bandaged side that was slightly exposed through the opening in his gown.

"The hell I'm not," Nick said, his face flushed with anger. The rage was not directed at Jones, but more at his current condition.

"Anaya and I are going to head back to headquarters. Call when you find out when they're releasing you and we'll come pick you up," Jones said.

"I'm still in this. Don't count me out," Nick said, grinding his teeth.

"Get some rest," Anaya said, giving a wink.

The two walked out into the pale light of the hallway and Nick grabbed his phone from the tray next to his bed. In his other hand, the black computer chip held between his thumb and forefinger.

Before he could pull up his contacts to make his intended call, the phone in his hand rang.

"Jesus Nick, I can't leave you alone for a damn minute!" Declan boomed through the phone's receiver.

"Deck, what the hell? How did you know to come?" Nick asked, struggling to understand how Declan Enright had come to the conclusion to drive to Texas.

"Truth be told, we were already on our way out to see you," Declan said.

"Hey tough guy, you had us worried," Izzy said.

Her voice was more muffled than Declan's, indicating that he was holding the phone that was obviously on speaker. Her voice was a welcomed sound. And the tone was much better than that of their last conversation.

"Aw, this is nothing. I almost lost an arm once," Nick said, trying to play the tough-guy role. An unnecessary display of bravado to the girl who'd applied the tourniquet that saved his arm, and his life.

"What am I going to do with you?" Izzy retorted, sighing audibly in the backdrop.

"Do you need me to give you two some alone time," Declan chided.

Izzy tried to ignore the taunt as Declan punctuated his statement by giving an overt wink. She pressed down hard on the pedal, accelerating the Camry past the morning flow of traffic. Izzy rolled her eyes and fought to keep a smile from cresting her lips.

"Alright, let's cut to the business at hand. Who did this to you and where can I find him?" Declan said, intensity replacing his light-hearted candor.

"Don't know. Big guy with a bald head. That's about as much of it as I can remember," Nick muttered.

His fist balled and the heartbeat monitor revealed the steady incremental rise. His elevated heart rate was in sync with his anger. He felt as useless as most of the witness he'd interviewed during his investigations. Nick breathed out heavily, trying desperately to calm himself so that he could to recall something useful.

"Okay. Who are you working the case with?" Izzy asked, assuming that in the interim since Nick's hospitalization some potential leads may have been generated.

"Kemper Jones. He's a detective with APD," Nick said.

"What about the female?" Izzy asked.

Nick thought he noted a trace of annoyance in her question.

"Oh, I assume you mean Anaya Patel?" Nick asked and then added, "She's with Child Protective Services. She said that you had called earlier this morning while I was recovering?"

"She answered your phone when I called," Izzy said.

Nick could tell that this bothered Izzy, but he wasn't completely sure why. Anaya was just helping with the case. Izzy shouldn't care anyway. She had moved on. She had Bill now. That's what she told him during their last conversation. Nick chewed on some ice chips to help distract this train of thought. The crunch drowned out the annoying jealous rantings of the voice inside his head.

"Anaya's good people," Nick said, throwing out the words Izzy used when she described Bill. He knew that it was childish but couldn't help himself.

The room got awkwardly silent before Declan interjected, "We want to help. But we're not going to be there officially."

Nick processed this and then asked, "You said you guys were already on your way out here? Why?"

"We were worried about you," Izzy said.

"And, apparently, rightly so," Declan added.

"I know there's no point in trying to talk you two out of it," Nick said.

"You got that right," Declan chuckled. Then he added, "We should be in this evening. Maybe sooner. Izzy drives like an asshole. We'll call when we're close."

"See you then," Nick said, ending the call.

The doctor entered and gave Nick a welcoming smile. His mannerisms contrasted with the nurse who'd been in earlier. He saw that Nick had his phone in hand and stopped.

"Would you like me to come back in a few minutes?"

"I'm all set with the call, thanks," Nick mumbled.

"Okay, then. The damage wasn't as bad as we initially thought. You were bleeding heavily so we sent you straight into the O.R." The doctor said; his voice was engaging, and he had a good bedside manner. He added, "Normally we would send you in for a CAT scan but, under the circumstances, we bypassed that and sent you in for surgery."

Nick nodded his receipt of the information.

"The knife's blade missed any vital organs. We packed the wound and bandaged your side." The doctor gave a contented smile.

"So, how long until I'm out of here?" Nick asked, cutting right to the chase.

"We'll keep you for observation. Maybe only for a day, but you're stable. I would say that we could have you out of here tomorrow morning. You're going to have some pain and discomfort for a while," the doctor said.

"I'm used to that," Nick responded, rubbing the old injury to his arm and then adding, "Tomorrow morning isn't going to work for me."

"You're going to be out of commission for a while during the healing process," the doctor added, coming to the realization that his patient was planning a speedy return to work. He continued, "You may not feel too much in the way of pain right now, but that is due to the low-dose morphine drip in your IV. I will prescribe something to help you manage the pain when you leave."

"That won't be necessary," Nick said, flatly.

There was no macho bravado in the statement. He refused to take anything stronger than an ibuprofen, regardless of the pain. His brother's PTSD had been worsened by an addiction to pain meds. Nick was convinced that the combination drove him to end his life. He never wanted to put himself in a similar situation.

"I'm going to let you rest. I'll see you in the morning before your release," the doctor said.

"Doc, I don't know how much you know about what I am working on, but a young girl's life is at stake. If you're telling me that my injury is stabilized, then I need to be discharged immediately." Nick was terse but calm.

"I'll see what I can do," the doctor replied.

"Do better than that," Nick pleaded.

"This will be against my recommendation, but I will begin the discharge paperwork. Give me an hour or so and I should have you moving toward that door," the doctor said flatly, giving into the agent's request.

"Thank you," Nick said.

"You're a brave man. The world could use more like you. Just don't go getting yourself killed."

The doctor exited the room, closing the door behind him.

Chapter 38

The morning brought with it a stiffness unlike anything he'd felt in recent years. Cain embraced the sensation. A reminder of his shortcomings during the previous night. A reminder of the kindness of the Pastor, allowing him another opportunity to serve as The Hand. He'd hoped that, after this was completed, he would be rewarded by an opportunity to see the Pastor in person. It had been a long time. The Pastor sent him CDs with his sermons, but to feel his embrace and hear his words while face-to-face was like being in the presence of God himself.

He put the selfish thoughts out of his head and focused on the task that lay ahead. The warehouse and makeshift hospital had also become his hotel room. But he did not require much. The surgeon was gone, as he'd assumed he would be. The table where his wounds were treated became his bed. In the light that fell from the warehouse's high windows, Cain took in the amenities. He could make out a toilet and sink in the corner.

Cain sat up, resting the weight of his massive body on his right arm. His neck protested the movement and pain radiated. The bullet now removed from his thigh did little to lessen the discomfort as he slid it over the edge of the table. Cain gingerly stepped down onto the cold concrete of the slab floor. Favoring his good side, he shuffled over to the door-less bathroom. He stared at his image through the filth-covered mirror.

His shirt was stained, and his body was covered in a combination of crusted blood and iodine. Cain set to work, dampening his undershirt and using it as a towel to wipe himself clean. It was a slow process, hampered by his current condition. The duffle-bag he'd brought with him was on the floor by the table. He ambled back and rifled through, gathering a fresh set of clothes. Cain rolled all of the blood-covered clothes into the sheet that had been draped over the table and hoisted it over his good shoulder. Grabbing the duffle, he walked out of the warehouse to the gray Ford Escape parked in the alley where the Range Rover had been.

There was a large dumpster in the recesses of the alley, just past the SUV. He dropped the duffle by the Ford and continued toward the trash bin. He tossed the sack of stained clothes into the rusted interior. He could hear the claws of the rats scratching at the metallic surface as they scurried to avoid the dumpster's newest arrival. Cain closed the heavy plastic lid and walked away, returning to the car.

Cain had been through similar ordeals in past service to the Pastor and knew that this was his new vehicle. The other one would be cleaned and reassigned, if not gutted and burned. Either way, it would never be used by him again. The door was unlocked, and the keys were tucked under the lip of the steering column. Always in the same place. Cain knew that the plates would be registered to him. To the name on his driver's license: Kyle Jenkins. An arbitrary association of letters that meant nothing to him. It was a clean name. One that allowed him the ability to move among the heathens without notice.

Cain gave a sigh of relief as he looked to the passenger seat and saw his large CD storage case. It was the only worldly possession that he clung to and without them he was lost. He sat in the driver's seat, allowing a moment for his body to adjust to the position. He pulled out his phone and opened the application.

He stared at the screen in disbelief. Cain manipulated that screen, pressing his fingers outward and zooming into the location of the Heathen. His mind was frantic. What he was seeing didn't make any sense and he let out a frustrated scream that reverberated in the quiet interior of the Ford.

The beacon showed that the Heathen was on the move, traveling north of Dallas. She was at least four hours ahead of him. He was angry at himself for allowing the post-surgery respite. Cain dug his right index finger into the dressing on his left bicep, allowing for the pain to release his frustration.

He grabbed a granola bar and bottle of water from his duffle bag. He was woozy from the warehouse surgery and needed to add some calories. Cain washed down a mouthful and slipped the car into drive, pulling out into the whirlwind downtown of Austin's Monday morning commuters.

"It's been a while," Jay said, recognizing Nick's number and answering it on the second ring.

"It sure has," Nick said to his friend.

"These days I get a little nervous when I see your number," Jay said.

The comment was made in jest, but there was a truth behind that statement.

"I'm back in Texas," Nick said.

"I know." There was a silence that followed.

Jay knew a lot of things. He had a network of informational resources at his disposal. Jay's skill in the intelligence world had served Nick well numerous times in the past.

"Every time you call me things get a little dicey. Especially, when you're in Texas."

"I'm working on something and I need your help," Nick said, regretting that the two only talked when circumstances dictated. Their friendship was now one driven by need.

"So, this is a business call?" Jay said, bypassing the nostalgic walk down memory lane.

"Yup," Nick said, wincing as he moved to reposition.

"You alright?" Jay asked, registering the grunting sound made by Nick.

"I took a knife to the gut last night," Nick said, nonchalantly.

"You're like a crash-test dummy," Jay said, chuckling softly at his own joke. He continued, "Seriously, what have you gotten yourself into this time?"

"I stumbled across a human trafficking case. It's international. They're moving young girls in from Mexico," Nick said, covering the details quickly so that he could get Jay up to speed on the reason for the call.

"Jesus. How old?" Jay asked.

"They're young. The youngest that we've come across today is between nine and eleven," Nick said.

"I don't know how you do it," Jay said, with disgust.

"Somebody has to."

It was a line that Nick had used in response to this typical reaction. Even the hardest of cops steered away from these kinds of cases. It took a special breed. It took people like Nick and Kemper Jones.

"I'll do whatever I can to help you. What do you need?" Jay asked.

After their last few experiences together, he had little doubt that his CIA friend would back down.

"We found what looks like some type of microchip embedded under the skin near their hip."

"Describe it to me." Jay was all in.

"It's small. About the size of my thumbnail. It is black but encased in a clear plastic. No markings that I can make out," Nick replied and then added, "I'll send you some pics when we hang up."

"Okay. I'm guessing that you want me to see what I can do with it?" Jay asked, stating the obvious.

"I think it's some sort of tracking device. I want you to see if you or someone you know can access the data on this," Nick said.

"Without me getting it in the hands of someone I trust, I won't know for sure what I can do," Jay said. He never gave false promises.

"How am I going to get it to you?" Nick asked.

"I'll send someone. Where are you and how long will you be there?" Jay asked.

"I'm at the Dell Seton Medical Center in downtown Austin and I'm only going to be here for another hour or so," Nick said, optimistically.

"I'll see what I can do," Jay said.

"I hate to look a gift horse in the mouth, but I'm going to need you to expedite this. A girl is on the run and the asshole who tried to give me the harry carry is still out there." Nick did not elaborate. Jay would understand the implication.

"Okay. If this is a tracking chip, then we may have some options," Jay said, pausing before adding, "Tell me you're not alone on this one."

"I've got some good people out here and, believe it or not, Declan and Izzy are on their way," Nick said, confidently.

"Good to hear," Jay said. "I'm sending someone to pick up the chip. He should be there before you're discharged," Jay said.

"You work fast," Nick said, sounding genuinely impressed.

"Like you said, I'm expediting," Jay said, ending the phone call.

Nick knew that his friend did not waste time with small talk, especially when time was of the essence. With Mouse on the run and the bald guy unaccounted for, time was definitely not on their side.

Chapter 39

The vibration in his pocket pulled him out of his light sleep. Retrieving the phone, Declan looked down at the caller ID: Val. He stretched, sat up, and then answered.

"Hey babe, everything okay?" Declan asked, knowing that she did not typically call unless it was something urgent.

They did not define their love with a need to maintain constant contact. The occasional text message was exchanged but typically calls were reserved for emergencies.

"Sorry to route my call through your wife's number, but I wanted to guarantee that you would answer," the male voice said.

Declan was paralyzed with fear. Someone from the Seven had come for his family. With the debt left unsettled, it was something that gnawed at the back of his mind. The words of Khaled the Translator's last threat echoed to this day. A threat against his family: *"Your house will burn and collapse on top of them."*

"If you so much as look at my family funny, then I will bring a world of pain upon you like you've never known," Declan said, spitting the words.

"I'm sure you would, but I'm a friend. Well, I'm Nick's friend," the voice said, calmly.

"I don't understand," Declan said, still reeling from the sudden thought of his wife and children's compromised safety.

"I helped you before with Khaled, but we never met," Jay said, allowing time for Declan to process this new information. He continued, "Like I said, I routed my call through your wife's number. I needed to ensure that you answered. I am truly sorry for giving you a scare."

Declan sighed, returning to his steady demeanor. Declan asked, "What's going on?"

"I'm worried that Nick's in real trouble," Jay said.

"He is. That's why we're heading out his way. He was stabbed last night," Declan said.

"I know. We just got off the phone," Jay said, calmly.

"Then what do you know that I don't?" Declan asked, confused.

"He told me that the girls he's trying to help may have microchips implanted. I have someone already on the way to retrieve one for analysis. That's bad news. He's up against some heavy hitters if that's the case," Jay said, relaying the information.

"Shit," Declan whispered.

The conversation caught the attention of Izzy who was busy slipping in and out of traffic, never allowing the Camry's speed to drop below 80 miles per hour. She could have been a race car driver.

"I'm glad that you are heading out there. He's in over his head," Jay said, allowing his concern to bleed through.

"He's been up against some tough odds before and came through," Declan said.

"True." Jay hesitated before continuing, "That's not the only thing I'm worried about."

"What do you mean?" Declan said, confused again.

"I know your background. I'm fully aware that you're capable of keeping a secret, but this goes beyond that. What I'm going to tell you compromises a promise I made to Nick years ago, but I feel that you need to understand some things so that you can help him," Jay said, in a constrained tone.

"Go on," Declan said, evenly.

His past had made him a lockbox of secrets. Details of missions tucked deep in his mind. One of the last men left standing from a unit that never existed. He could handle whatever this man had to say.

"He asked for my help a few years back. Before the Khaled incident. He was in Texas and working a case not too different from the one he's on now. It was definitely a lower-tiered organization of child peddlers," Jay said.

"Okay," Declan said, waiting.

"Nick had worked his ass off linking the members of the organization to the exploited children. He brought charges down on everyone that he could loosely affiliate with the trafficking of these kids," Jay said.

"Sounds good so far, but I feel that you're not done," Declan muttered.

"Correct. Things fell apart in court. The upper echelon of the organization was able to lawyer their way out free and clear while the low-end members took the fall," Jay said, laying the groundwork.

"Sometimes that's the way things break. You can beat the rap, but you can't beat the ride," Declan said, quoting a line he'd used a thousand times over in the past.

"True, but Nick didn't see it that way. He couldn't let it go. And that's where I came in. He went off the reservation," Jay said, quietly adding, "And I helped him."

"What do you mean? We're talking about the same Nick? The boy scout and poster child for professionalism?" Declan asked.

"Using assets at my disposal we tracked the men down. He developed a plan and I assisted in gathering as much intel as possible. You know the game. It was like being overseas again. Schedules, security, location scouting, etcetera," Jay said, trailing off.

"And then?" Declan said, anxious.

"Nick took them out. The three that had avoided prosecution and two members of their security detail."

Jay allowed time for Declan to process this information. He waited patiently for the former operator to digest it, knowing that if anyone could take news like this in stride and without judging, it would be Declan Enright.

"It sounds like Nick did what most of us would never have the balls to," Declan said, providing his stamp of approval.

"That's true. There is a special place in hell for pedophiles and anyone that sells children into the sex trade. That's why I was willing to help. But I saw what it did to him. You only knew the man after. I witnessed the transformation," Jay said.

"He seems like he dealt with those demons as well as anyone," Declan countered.

"I guess, but at the time it ruined him. He lost his wife to it. He became a recluse, burying himself in cases. His father's death and mother's dementia turned out to be a blessing in disguise. It pulled him out of his funk," Jay said, troubled by exposing his friend's weaknesses.

"And you're worried that it's going to happen again?" Declan asked, understanding the reason for the call.

"Yes. I'm not sure that if he slips again he'll recover," Jay said, concern saturating his words.

"But you're still planning on helping him with the microchip?" Declan asked.

"Yes. I'm hoping that you will be able to figure out a solution that doesn't ruin our friendship," Jay said, with an uneasy finality.

"I've already planned a solution for the bald asshole that turned Nick into a pincushion." There was no subtlety to the statement. It was resolute.

"That's what I figured since you and your partner are not on the clock," Jay said, further revealing his ability to gather intel.

"What you shared, stays with me," Declan said.

"I appreciate it," Jay said, acknowledging his trust in Declan's words.

"What should I call you?" Declan asked.

There was no response and then the call ended.

Izzy looked over at Declan as he pocketed the cell phone. Her eyebrows raised and the expression on her face was easily decoded. She waited expectantly for the details from the last call, only hearing one side of it.

"We'd better make up some time." Declan said without looking at Izzy.

He knew that this response would not satisfy her, but it was the best he could offer up.

They drove on in silence and he pondered the call. Nick wasn't as squeaky clean as he'd thought.

Declan took comfort in knowing that he wasn't the only one with secrets.

Chapter 40

The Ford moved with the flow of traffic. Cain made sure to stay within a mile or two of the speed limit. He wanted nothing more than to mash the pedal and chip away at the distance between his current location and the Heathen's. Patience was needed. Getting pulled over could create a series of unwanted events. His GPS rerouted to accommodate for any changes to the red blips direction. Cain had made up some distance when the Heathen stopped for half an hour in Texarkana, but he was still over three hours behind. He soothed his anxiety with the Pastor's words. The sermon stirred him and provided a needed distraction.

It will call to you in different ways. It will seek to find weakness. The Devil will try to penetrate the chink in your spiritual armor. How do you harden yourself to these attacks? How do you block an invisible blade that seeks to slash at your belief? Acceptance! That is the answer. Acceptance that you are not as strong as you think! Acceptance that you have weakness! Acceptance that you are not worthy! It is in that subjugation that you will find a new strength. You will feel God's embrace. Lower yourself so that you can be raised up anew!

Cain rubbed the bandaged wound near his neck. He smiled, embracing the Pastor's message.

Her body was sore. The explosive tension that she'd applied to keep herself wedged during the car crash left her stiff. The eight hours curled in the rear seat of the bus only added to it. She stretched and rolled her neck in an effort to loosen up. She stared out at the landscape.

Her heart leaped when she saw the sign welcoming her to Arkansas. Mouse was out of Texas. The thought made her smile. She wasn't exactly sure what her plan was once she got to Pidgeon, but she'd figure it out. In the hum of the bus's engine, she allowed herself to daydream about the next chapter in her life. Something she hadn't done in years. For the first time in a long time, she felt like she had something to look forward to.

Chapter 41

"What?" Nick asked, shocked at the statement.

"The beacons are everywhere!" Jay exclaimed. Not one to get emotionally invested in the relay of information, he calmed and then continued, "My tech was able to follow the data trail and link to the site where the information from the chip was being sent. Without divulging much about the process, he was able to access the database and view it from the user's point of view."

"I'm totally impressed. So, you can find the girl?" Nick asked, hopefully.

"That's what I'm saying. The screen looks like a goddamned Christmas tree. They've got these chips in a lot of girls," Jay said. The reality of his comment was overwhelming.

"So how do we find her? And we've got to figure out what to do with all the others," Nick said, sounding desperate.

"I focused my efforts on the girl you're looking for. I gave the tech the grid coordinates of your apartment. We had the timeline of when she was there, so it was relatively easy once he figured out how to manipulate the system," Jay said, excited at the prospect.

"And?"

"Each chip has its own tag. Your girl's is MX1249. I'm not sure of its meaning, but I'm guessing that the MX represents Mexico. Maybe they tag their girls by place of origin. I'm not sure and right now that doesn't really matter." Jay caught his breath and continued, "My guy created a way for you to track her in real time. I've texted you a link."

"Fantastic!" Nick said.

"Not so fast. She's in Arkansas and moving north." The implications of this were not good.

"Arkansas?" Nick thought about the possibilities and didn't like the prospects. He added, "They must've grabbed her while I was stuck in the hospital. I have no idea where they could be headed, but at least we've got a better chance now that we can pinpoint her location. I just hope we're not too late."

"I'll keep you updated on my end," Jay said, ending the call.

Jones, Rusty, and Anaya sat in the conference room at APD headquarters and stared at Nick. Only hearing half of the conversation, but surmising its gist.

"I've got two questions. Was I right about it being a tracking chip? And two, how the hell did'ya get that info so damn quickly?" Jones asked, raising his eyebrows in suspicion at the second inquiry as he slipped into a deep Texas drawl.

"Yes, you were right about the chip," Nick said, avoiding the second question altogether.

"Ideas?" Nick asked the group. His body positioning in the chair favored his injured left side.

"Maybe State Police could help? Assuming she's on the highway." It was Rusty who spoke now.

"Good point. We've got a description of the bald guy's vehicle. But we're assuming that he has her. And assuming that he's still using the Range Rover," Jones said.

"That's a lot of assumptions, but it's better than what we had a few minutes ago," Nick said.

"At least we know that she's probably alive," Anaya said, speaking for the first time in a while.

"How do we know that?" Rusty asked.

"Because she's still moving. If not, then I'm guessing they'd have dumped her somewhere," Nick said, nodding his head as if reassuring himself that he was right.

"Good point. I'm going to get in touch with Arkansas State Police and see if we can get someone to intercept." Jones stepped up and walked to his desk.

Nick was silent for a moment and then put his phone to his ear. "Where are you?"

"Um, we're still in Tennessee. We lost a little time to some road construction." Declan realized that there was more to the question and asked, "Why? What's up?"

"How far are you from Memphis?" Nick asked, intently.

Declan looked at the GPS on Izzy's phone and said, "Hour and a half, tops. Again, why?"

"We've got a lock on the girl. She's heading your way," Nick said, excitement filling his voice.

"Where are you?" Declan asked.

"There's no way we can make up the time. Maybe once she stops moving we might be able to get a flight out, but I have a bad feeling that we are operating on borrowed time," Nick said.

Nick didn't need to add any detail to the statement's meaning. Everyone in the group was well aware of the stakes.

"Alright, we've got this," Declan said, confidently.

"Sorry to put you in this position. I wish I could do it myself, but..." Nick never finished the sentence.

"I know." Declan hated the seriousness of Nick's tone. Especially in light of recent information. He lightened the tone and added, "It's time you let the varsity team play."

A little chuckle escaped Nick as his friend's cockiness created some levity. "Okay, just remember who saved your ass last time."

"Um, I'm right here," Izzy said, in the background.

Her sarcastic tone caused Nick to smile. At the same moment, his eyes caught Anaya's and he noticed what appeared to be a trace of jealousy at the banter.

"I'm going to send you a link. It'll allow you the ability to track Mouse's position. I'm also going to send you a photo. It's a little grainy. It's from a convenience-store camera, but you should be able to identify her from it," Nick said, returning the conversation back to the business at hand.

"Mouse?" Declan asked.

"Yup. She's tiny, but don't let her size fool you. She is as tough as they come," Nick replied.

"I like her already," Izzy said.

"Be safe. If she's with the guy from my apartment, then take precautions. He's dangerous," Nick said.

"So am I."

Declan let that comment hang in the air for a moment before clicking the end button.

"State has all the information. They're going to set some units up on I40 and look for the Range Rover. They'll keep me posted," Jones said, re-entering the room.

"As soon as she's safe we're going to need to figure out how to help the rest of the girls," Nick said, scanning the room.

"I agree, but let's focus on finding Mouse first and go from there," Jones said.

"I think that you should be resting," Anaya said, looking at Nick sitting uncomfortably and favoring his injured side.

"There's no way I'm going to lie down and take a nap while that asshole is hunting a little girl," Nick said, intensely.

"No point in arguing with his stubborn ass. I think I'm the only one left in this state that will work with him. Hell, why d'ya think he has to slum it with us city cops? His Bureau buddies can't keep up," Jones said, laughing.

Nick smiled at the group but couldn't help feeling the not-so-subtle truth in Jones's remark.

Chapter 42

She moved quickly through the herd of people that were meandering outside. A few of the passengers lit cigarettes. They stood waiting for their bags to be offloaded from the undercarriage. Her ticket itinerary said that this was a transfer to the 1214 Bus. There was a little over an hour at the station.

Mouse went directly to the bathroom. She'd used the privacy of toilet on the bus but wanted to organize the cash in her backpack, worried that someone might find it odd that a girl of her age would have a wad of money. She slipped a twenty-dollar bill into her pocket and zipped the sack up.

The station wasn't very big, and it felt smaller with the crowd. Some were huddled on the floor with their cell phones connected to a wall plug. A man shuffled past her whose smell reminded her of the drunk that had helped her get the ticket. Mouse made for a place serving hot food. There was no name above the enclave, just a sign that read Open 24 Hours. She ordered a burger, hot dog, and French fries. Her stomach rumbled as the scent wafting off the grill entered her nose. The Powerbars and Gatorade had sufficed up to this point, but her body yearned for real food. What better way to embrace America than through their greasy staples.

Mouse found a small aluminum table by a large fake plant. Using her hand to clear of the crumbs from the last visitor, she then laid out her feast. The only thought in her head was *"Which one should I eat first?"* She committed and gripped the burger with two hands, breathing through her nose as she began devouring like a shark in blood-filled water. She paused only long enough to shovel a few fries into her mouth.

It had been a long time since Mouse could say that she was happy. It was an elusive concept under the circumstances of her life. But right now, right here, in the Greyhound bus station in Memphis, she felt it. Or what she perceived was the closest thing to happiness that she'd experienced since her mother's death.

Leaning back, surveying the pile of grease and mustard stained wrappers, she rubbed her belly, contented. Looking at the itinerary, she did the math. Only twenty-two more hours and she would be in Saginaw.

And then on to Pidgeon. On to her new life.

Chapter 43

The group sat watching the blip update position. There seemed to be a lag time, and Nick guessed this was because Jay's tech support was sending them a hacked signal.

"This is killing me," Nick said through gritted teeth.

"Don't I know it," Jones said. "Good thing is we've got a lock on her. Only a matter of time now."

Nick nodded and slowly stood. The meds from the hospital had run their course, and the dullness of the pain was gone. Sitting unmoved in the chair, it felt like a vice gripped his side. But standing up was like the knife was being plunged back in again.

"Easy, Nick," Anaya said, swooping in to assist. "Why don't we find you someplace more comfortable?"

"Nah, I need to move around a bit. I'm gonna grab some water," Nick said. He was stilted and not able to stand erect, so his tall frame seemed stunted.

"There's a fresh pot of coffee in the break room. I'm gonna contact dispatch and see where we're at with the troopers. Looks like we've got to reach out to Tennessee now," Jones said, already moving to the door.

"Sounds better than water," Nick said, forcing a smile.

"I'll be outside for a bit. I've gotta let Jasper stretch his legs," Rusty said.

"Hey Rusty, you and your partner can cut loose for a while. I'll hit you up if we need your services," Jones said.

"Nope, I'd rather stay close. Seems, every time I leave, y'all call me right back. I'm gonna ride this out," Rusty said with a cock of his head.

The group temporarily separated. Nick took small steps and the walk to the break room seemed a marathon's distance. Anaya followed, keeping his slow pace. She smiled at his efforts and kept her hand near the small of his back. Not touching him, but prepared to react if he needed. She looked like a parent hovering over their toddler as the first steps were taken.

"I'm fine," Nick said.

"I didn't say you weren't. Can't a girl get a cup of coffee?" Anaya jested, sarcastically.

"Sorry, I just hate being a lame duck," Nick said with an uncharacteristic timidity.

"There's nothing lame about you," Anaya said playfully.

"Says you," Nick said. He changed the subject, adding, "So, I never really got a chance to thank you before."

"Thank me? For what?" Anaya asked.

"For saving my life. If it wasn't for you and Mouse, I'd most likely be dead," Nick said, humbly.

"Oh that. Geesh, that was nothing," Anaya said, feigning bashfulness.

"You ever shot a gun before?" Nick asked, genuinely.

"Why? Did I do bad?" Anaya asked coyly.

"Not at all. Under the circumstances, you did great! It's harder than people realize. You shot at a moving target in the dark and hit him. Best part was you didn't hit me," Nick said, giving her a kind smile.

"I was actually aiming for you. Thank God I'm such a lousy shot," Anaya said, laughing at her own joke.

Nick chuckled, but the pain struck him like a sledgehammer and caused him to stop.

"How'd you get into all this?" Nick asked.

"All what? Social work?"

"Yeah. From what Jones tells me, you're the go-to person around here on cases like this," Nick said, paying forward the compliment.

"I guess you could say it's my calling. Someone helped me out of a bad situation a long time ago, and ever since that day, I knew this was something that I had to do," Anaya said, instantly regretting the exposure to her past.

"How bad?" Nick didn't want to pry but was fascinated by the woman and wanted to know more.

"I don't usually talk about it, but let's just say that Mouse and I aren't so different," Anaya said softly. She then added, "Well there's one glaring difference. She's ten times tougher than I ever was."

"I'd say you're pretty damn tough," Nick said. His cheeks flushed at his cheesy attempt at a compliment. He knew his delivery did little to bely its flirtatious undertones.

Anaya smiled and busied herself at the counter of the breakroom, pouring the coffee.

"I don't even know where to begin with the other girls on that map," Nick said, easing back from the last comment.

"I think, right now, it's important to focus on Mouse. Once she's safe, we can figure out the next step," Anaya said. She was pensive for a moment before she added, "One thing I do know is that, the first indication that they get that we're on to them, and they will change tactics. This is why they're so hard to catch."

"I know. That's my fear. These groups are always two steps ahead of us. We usually only catch the sloppy ones," Nick said, glumly.

Chapter 44

The overhead speaker crackled, and the boarding announcement for the 1214 bus was barely audible over the noise of other travelers. Her full belly had brought on a weariness that she hadn't felt in a while. The adrenaline dump that had fueled her for the past few days had vacated. Mouse was left with a strong desire to sleep. That's what she planned to do as soon as she got on the bus.

There was a slow gaggle of people making their way toward the side exit that would bring them to the bus departure area. Mouse moved quickly, wanting to ensure that she secured a seat in the rear again. She exited the air-conditioned building and was smacked with the heavy humidity of the Tennessee air. The smell of diesel fuel was overwhelming and caused her to cough. As she fell in line with the other passengers, something caught her eye. It was something in the movement, a directness that seemed out of place.

Mouse turned and saw him approaching. He was closing the gap quickly. Terrified. Caught in her momentary lapse of contentedness, she'd let her guard down. Frantic, she looked for an escape. She opened her mouth to scream.

"Mouse!" the man yelled.

Hearing her name caused her to pause, stopping the scream before it began. Perplexed, she stood frozen by indecision.

"It's okay! We're here to help," a woman's voice shouted.

The woman appeared, stepping into sight from behind the man. She had dark hair and tanned skin. They both stopped approximately ten feet away and put their hands out. The two looked like they were trying to calmly approach a stray dog. Unsure and cautious.

"We're friends with Nick and Anaya. We're here to help you," Izzy said reassuringly.

Mouse looked around nervously, her eyes ping-ponging between the approaching pair and the bus she was about to board. She'd never seen these two people before. They knew her name, but life had taught her many lessons. Trust was not given easily.

She looked toward the bus and then back at the two, who had stopped their slow approach. Some of the other passengers had taken notice of this odd exchange, not knowing what to make of it.

The man had kind eyes, but the rest of him looked like he was cut from stone, standing rigid as if ready to pounce. She heard her father's words. *Commit to the action needed. Then act.* The problem was Mouse could not make a decision.

And then something strange happened. The stone man slapped at his neck as if reacting to a bee sting. Seconds later, he crumpled to the ground. The woman next to him panicked, dropping to her knees to render aid. He lay on the ground, unmoving.

"Declan! What the..." Izzy couldn't finish the statement.

She dropped to her knees next to Declan. Someone appeared beside her. Izzy moved for her sidearm, which was concealed under her untucked shirt.

"I'm a doctor! Is this your husband?" he asked.

He took up a position alongside her and rapidly moved his hands along his neck, checking for a pulse. He bent low putting his right ear just above Declan's mouth as he looked for the rise and fall of his chest.

"Huh? What? No. Not his wife. You're a doctor?" Izzy jumbled the barrage of questions.

"Relax. He has a pulse and he's breathing. Any history?" the doctor asked.

He sat up and pulled a phone from his pocket.

"I...I don't know," Izzy stammered.

Their plan to recover the girl was quickly falling apart. Izzy shot a glance toward the girl. She was still standing in the same spot. Frozen in place. Izzy held up a finger toward that girl, indicating for her to wait while she figured out what to do with her fallen partner.

"Yes. Hello. I've got a man unconscious. He's got a pulse and is breathing. Please step it up," the doctor said into the phone. He ended the call and turned to Izzy. "Good news, there is an ambulance close by. Should be here in a minute."

"What the hell is going on?" Izzy asked.

"Not sure. Looks like a bee sting," the doctor said.

He directed Izzy's attention, pointing to a small red dot along the right side of Declan's neck. There was a tiny drop of blood and the skin around it was raised slightly.

"Is your friend allergic?"

"I don't know. Shit! Bee sting?" Izzy asked. The question was more to herself than the doctor.

A loud siren filled the air as an ambulance rounded the corner. The blue and red lights bounced off the windows of the bus terminal creating a disco tech effect.

"Jesus, that was fast," Izzy said, looking in the direction of the noise.

"Well, the lady on the phone did say that they were just around the corner," the doctor said, reassuringly.

He then stood and began waving his arms overhead, flagging down the ambulance. He pointed down at Declan as the ambulance pulled along the curb.

In the commotion, Izzy looked back toward Mouse or where she used to be. The girl was gone and so was the bus. Izzy pulled out her phone as the two large EMTs approached purposefully, wheeling a gurney between them.

"Something happened to Declan! Bee sting. He just collapsed. The girl is on the move. Keep tracking her! I'll figure this out. They're prepping him to move," Izzy said in rapid fire succession to Nick.

She hung up without waiting for a response and addressed the medical team. Izzy lifted her shirt just enough to expose her badge that was clipped to her beltline. They nodded to her, indicating that they got the message.

"I'll follow. Where are you taking him?" Izzy asked one of the paramedics as he loaded Declan onto a gurney.

"Memorial," the man said, strapping in Declan's chest.

"Thank you," Izzy said to the doctor before running off toward the parking lot.

Cain had planned it. He would wait until the Heathen was in line for the bus and then approach. His lines rehearsed, he would have acted like a thankful parent finding his runaway daughter. If she resisted, then any onlookers would understand. It would be perceived as a father trying to recover his rebellious teen. The gun pressed against her side would quickly calm her down, and he would extricate her to his Ford Escape. Quick and easy.

In a moment of chaos, it all fell apart. Just as he'd begun moving toward the Heathen, someone called out to her. A man and woman had known where she was. They were there to intercept her.

This man and woman knew exactly where she was. *How was that possible?* And then, in the midst of their intrusion, the man collapsed. There were so many things wrong with what Cain had just witnessed. His small window of opportunity had been stolen from him. Rage caused his hands to tremble as he watched the Heathen's bus pull out from the depot.

Chapter 45

Izzy broke into a sprint to the Camry as she saw that the ambulance was already pulling out of the bus terminal parking lot. She entered the car and dropped it into drive and accelerated to catch up. Pulling out her cellphone, she called Nick again. Her last message had been an onslaught of craziness and she wanted to clarify things.

"We saw the girl. Almost had her. Declan's in an ambulance, and we're heading to the hospital," Izzy said in rapid-fire succession.

"What? Declan's hurt?" Nick asked, wrought with guilt.

"Bee sting or something," Izzy said. The fog of confusion still evident in her disjointed explanation.

"I don't understand. Bee sting?" Nick asked.

"Strangest thing. We saw the girl as she was about to get on a Greyhound bus. We were talking to her, and then all of a sudden, Declan went down," Izzy said, slowing the pace of her words.

"The girl?" Nick asked.

"Gone. I'm assuming that she got on the bus. I was distracted by Declan's situation," Izzy said, expressing her frustration.

"At least we know that she is on a bus. We can get some local assistance and pick her up. Keep me posted on Declan's condition," Nick said.

"Thank goodness a doctor was standing by when he went down. Who would've thought that tough old Declan could be brought down by a bee sting?" Izzy paused as she spoke the words. Realizing the improbable likelihood of the occurrence, she froze.

"Crazy," Nick said.

Izzy didn't hear him. Her mind quickly replayed the events that just transpired.

"Izzy?" Nick asked.

"Shit! Gotta go. Keep me posted on the girl," Izzy said, hanging up the phone without waiting for a response.

The bus moved onto I57 heading north. Cain followed a few cars behind in his Ford Escape. The disappointment of the failed intercept at the bus station plagued his mind, causing him to press hard into his injured thigh. With the sharp pain came a temporary relief.

He would have to wait for the bus to stop again. He knew that his timeline had just been extended. A need to hear some reassurance from the Pastor overwhelmed him, but he refrained from relaying his latest missed opportunity. Instead, he inserted a new CD and allowed the words to provide the comfort, like that of a worn blanket.

It is in the deepest moments of desperation that we seek his strength. For to turn your back at those times is a recipe for certain disaster. But don't be fooled. Another hand will reach out for you. That hand will feel familiar. It will give you hope, but then it will pull you deeper. Into that dark place. For the seeker of souls will use those moments of weakness to twist you. To confuse you.

How do you see the difference? How do you know which hand is the way? The answer is simple. In the darkness, you will feel that light cascade upon you. You will know because it will be brilliant.

As if on cue, the high-beams of a passing 18-wheeler momentarily blinded Cain. He smiled faintly, knowing he was on the right path.

Chapter 46

The red light seeped in through his eyes as they opened. He was moving and could feel the shake of the vehicle. On his back, he tried without success to sit upright. His chest was restrained. His wrists slid along a railing and were also secured. Declan replayed the events, and he recalled finding the girl, Mouse. He was talking with her, and then it all went dark.

Still dizzy from whatever caused him to blackout, he no longer fought against the restraints. Looking up, he saw a man wearing a light blue shirt with an EMS patch on the sleeve. The man was leaning forward and talking with the driver. It was hard to make out the conversation through the noise of the ambulance's rumbling. It was in the mannerism of the EMS worker that Declan noticed something was off, an intangible but defining quality in the man. He felt a wave of nervousness rush over him, and he began to wiggle his wrist, attempting to find a way to free himself from the restraint.

"How far out?" the man in the EMS said, shouting over the noise to the driver.

The answer was muffled, but it sounded like he said, *not long*. And then his voice became clear as he yelled, "What the hell is she doing?"

"Who?" the man in the EMS shirt said, not having a clear visual through the small window.

"The damn lady from the bus station! She's passing us," the driver said, nervously.

"So? She's probably trying to get to the hospital before us," the man in the EMS shirt said. He showed little concern and added, "Better for us, anyway, since we're not going to the hospital."

With that last comment, he turned to look back at Declan. Seeing that he was awake seemed to cause him to panic slightly.

"He's coming to," the man in the EMS shirt relayed.

"Not to worry. Those restraints are tight," the driver said.

It was obvious that the man in the EMS shirt was not convinced, and he shifted his body to the bench seat adjacent to Declan. He began checking the straps one at a time, starting with the chest. Hovering over Declan, he checked the far side wrist strap.

"Shit!" the driver yelled as he slammed the brakes, causing the ambulance to lurch forward hard.

The sudden movement caught the unbalanced man in the EMS shirt off-guard, sending him forward over Declan and into a hard metal cabinet above. The ambulance jerked violently to the right as more expletives escaped the mouth of the driver. The hard turn pitched the boxed vehicle to the left. It teetered, fitting against the inertia pulled. The burping sound of the skidding tires and then split second of silence before the ambulance crashed down on the driver's side. Declan was jostled hard, but the tight restraints and the floor-locked gurney proved to be his safeguard.

The screech of metal on asphalt was deafening as the ambulance slid on its side until it came to a stop. The tires were still spinning hard but without the street underneath they just made loud whirring sound.

The engine stopped and the noise from the wheels went silent. Declan craned his neck and saw the man in the EMS shirt pressed into a corner. He looked like a crumpled laundry heap, except for the bloodied face that protruded. His body had been folded into an unnatural state. Declan couldn't tell if he was dead, but he was definitely temporarily out of commission.

The crunch of glass under foot could be heard approaching. Someone was walking around the front of the ambulance.

"Hands! Show me slowly! Slower!" Izzy's voice was loud but controlled. "Keep 'em there and don't move!"

Declan heard the familiar metallic clink of handcuffs.

"Izzy, one's down in here. Not moving. Not sure his status," Declan said, calling out to his friend.

The rear door opened and made a loud crashing sound as it swung down onto the pavement. Izzy entered and looked at Declan suspended sideways on the gurney like a fly trapped in a spider's web. He was smiling.

Gun out, she moved past him and headed straight for the man in the EMS shirt. She pulled two pairs of zip ties from the small of her back. She went to work, securing his hands and ankles. She ran an additional tie to connect the restraints behind his back, effectively hog-tying him. The crumpled man grunted as Izzy ratcheted down the final tie, indicating that he was still among the living. She searched him and came up holding a gun she'd removed from his waistline.

"Healthcare ain't what it used to be," Declan said with a laugh.

"Are you just going to hang out all day or what?" Izzy asked as she unstrapped Declan's sinewy frame from the gurney.

As the straps came free he plunked down to landing on his hands and knees. He took a moment to orient himself before standing.

"How'd you know?" Declan asked.

"It happened fast. You going down, I mean. But as I was getting in the car to follow, I realized something was off. You going down with a bee sting and a doctor right there were clear red flags in hindsight. But the real *aha* moment came while I was driving behind the ambulance. I knew you were in trouble. That doctor called for an ambulance but never gave a location. Yet, moments later it appeared," Izzy said. "Sorry it took me so long to piece it together."

"Thank God you figured it out. I'm not sure things would've ended well for me if you hadn't," Declan said, rubbing at the friction burns on his wrists.

"I'm going to call this location into Nick and let him work out the details with local authorities. We can't be here when police show up. We need to find the girl, and getting tied into this ambulance crash is just going to slow us down," Izzy said, assuredly.

"Agreed," Declan said, hopping out of the crashed ambulance.

He looked at his phone. The red dot on the screen was on the move. He assumed that whoever intervened at the bus station wouldn't be far behind.

As he sat in the passenger seat of the blue Camry his eyes had a steely focus to them. Like the calm before a storm.

Chapter 47

The vibration of the bus had a soothing quality and was lulling Mouse toward sleep as the wave of adrenaline from the strange encounter at the Memphis bus terminal receded. She couldn't allow sleep. No chance that her guard would be let down again.

She went from row to row, scanning the bus's occupants, unable to discern friend or foe. Everyone around her was an unknown. It was an awful feeling to be surrounded by people but feel completely alone at the same time. It was in these moments that Mouse longed for her mother and father. She tried to fight the sudden upheaval of emotion. She was caught off-guard as a tear fell from her eye.

The sensation of the salty drop rolling down her cheek was a foreign one, and she could not recall the last time she'd shed one. But the release had caused an unsuspected chain reaction. Mouse pulled her feet up on the seat cushion and wrapped her arms tightly around her legs as if giving a hug. Rocking back and forth, she pressed her face into her thighs and let go. She cried silently for several minutes, allowing for her tough exterior to soften for a moment. It was a cathartic release.

Once the wave of sadness had passed, she wiped her face against her sleeve, removing any evidence of her exposed feelings. She tucked them back into the deep recesses of her heart, where they would return to their dormancy.

Her thoughts returned to the man and woman at the station. They called her by name. They knew Nick and Anaya. *It didn't matter. Nobody could protect her.* The bald man proved that. He was able to come for her when she was under their protection.

Poor Nick, she thought, wondering if he was still alive. The last time she'd seen him he was covered in blood with the bald man on top. She shivered at the image.

The bus began to slow. The hiss of the breaks as they engaged, protesting the work. They'd only left the Memphis station about half an hour ago. Not a good time to stop. Not with people so close behind. Then she saw the reason. The blue and red flashed alongside the windows, casting a strobed effect in the bus's interior. The passengers rumbled in excitement, twisting to see. Some protested quiet complaints as the bus crossed into the breakdown lane of the highway.

Mouse clutched her backpack tighter, seeking some comfort from the lumpy sack. The bus came to a complete stop, and the interior lights came to life, illuminating the cabin. A boom of thunder filled the air. Abruptly, the day's humidity gave way to an evening storm. Lightening filled the sky intertwining with the cruiser's strobes as the rain began to pour.

The driver pulled the lever, and the doors to the bus swung inward. A police officer wearing a light brown shirt and green pants entered. He had an olive drab green hat with a large, round brim. His clothes were soaked from the poorly timed rain, and his face didn't look pleasant. He seemed annoyed as the passengers at this inconvenience. He spoke briefly to the driver. Then he stood erect and faced the passengers. He looked from seat to seat and then glanced back at an image on his phone. The Trooper made eye contact with Mouse, and his face seemed to lose some of its rigidity. Some but not all.

He walked directly toward her, ignoring the stares and whispers from other passengers. He stopped at her row. Mouse was in the window seat and pretended not to notice the man as he bent down. He was a lean man with a tight jaw and short gray hair. He opened his mouth to speak. Mouse, half-expecting to hear a yell, cringed at the crackle of his voice.

"I'm Trooper Landers, and I'm here to help you," Landers said softly. His voice was a stark contrast to his wiry frame and tough exterior.

Mouse turned her head and looked at him but said nothing.

"It's okay. You've got some people very worried about you. Come with me, and we'll get you back home," Landers said, conveying a genuine concern for the small teen.

Mouse nodded. There was no point in arguing. It would be a lost cause.

Mouse slipped her arms into the straps of the backpack and exited her seat. She walked slowly through the aisle with her head down. The police officer followed behind, keeping his left hand on her shoulder. A gentle reminder not to run.

Trooper Landers thanked the bus driver, and he stepped off onto the shoulder of the road. Mouse stood in the rain and thought about running, but the large hand of the trooper squeezed her shoulder. He obviously anticipated this reaction. She shrugged her acceptance and placated the lawman. They walked toward the police car parked at the rear of the bus. The flashing lights were blinding and the downpour added to it. The trooper tipped his hat to deflect the blinding lights.

"Let's get you out of this god-awful rain," Landers said, gently guiding her forward.

Thunder boomed as lightning simultaneously lit the darkened sky. The Greyhound bus pulled away, continuing its journey north. She was being pulled back to her start point as she watched the brake lights of her future disappear down the road.

Trooper Landers' hand suddenly gripped her tightly and then released. Mouse looked back and saw him lying on his back clutching his neck. His legs flailed as he squirmed. A low gurgling sound came out of the man. The rain washed away the blood as soon as it emptied from his neck. Landers' hands clasped tightly at his throat, trying without avail to ebb the flow. His were eyes wide with panic as he gasped. No words followed. Death did not give the dying man a final goodbye.

Mouse turned from the fallen officer to look for the threat, but as she did, she was hoisted into the air. The grip clenched around her midsection like a vice, knocking the wind out of her. Her arms pinned, she flailed relentlessly. Mouse's writhing did little to release her constraints. She bucked her head, hoping to make contact with his nose or face but found the shoulder instead. Mouse buried her heel into his groin, but her kick had no effect. Not even a grunt of discomfort was uttered in response.

Past the cruiser was an SUV without any headlights on. Its silhouette was made visible as lightning shot sideways across the sky. She was carried to the passenger side, her body slammed to the ground, and she felt the man's impressive weight as he placed his knee in the center of her back. The force of it pushed the air from her lungs. Mouse turned her head to the side, fighting to breathe and got a mouthful of muddy water. Her arms were yanked behind her back, and she felt something bite at her wrists, pulling them together tightly. Hard to tell, but it felt like a rope or cord. There was no slack for her to manipulate her hands.

A click of a door opening, the massive hands grabbed her by the hair and legs. Mouse was painfully hoisted upward and tossed on the floorboard of the backseat. She landed hard, and with no hands to break her fall, she scraped her face along the floor mat, tasting blood. A heavy blanket covered her, blacking out the lightning filled sky.

The car drove off without any word from the man. Mouse lay in the shrouded darkness and tried to figure her next move. Her way out. She heard her father's words, *Focus. Visualize what you need to do.*

For the first time in a long time, she couldn't come up with a plan. For the first time in a long time, Mouse was truly terrified.

Chapter 48

"Well, it's official. Izzy is in charge of all the driving from this point forward," Declan said, talking into the speakerphone of his cell.

"If we keep letting her save our asses, then we're never going to live it down," Nick said, chuckling softly.

"Where are we meeting the trooper that located her?" Izzy asked, interrupting the banter.

"At their Memphis headquarters on Summer Ave. We're waiting for the confirmation when he's back in route," Jones interjected from the background.

"Well, we've been tracking Mouse's blip. It stopped briefly and started moving in the opposite direction. I'm assuming the trooper already has her," Declan said.

"We saw that too. You're probably right. There's a slight delay in communicating with the state police. Give me a second, and I'll make another call to verify," Jones said.

Nick took the phone off speaker and pressed it closer to his ear.

"Hey guys, are you okay? I feel really bad about putting you in this position. Never my intention."

"Don't ever apologize to me again. You'd do the same for us," Declan said seriously.

"Fair enough," Nick said. He was about to add to his comment when he heard Jones yell.

"What was that?" Declan asked, hearing the background noise on Nick's end.

"Hang on." Nick pulled the phone away from his face and then put it back on speaker. "You'd better hear this."

"Trooper's dead. They found him after he didn't respond. They contacted the Greyhound bus driver, who confirmed that the girl got off with the trooper. Our guess is that the doer has Mouse," Jones said, speaking rapidly. No drawl. No time for theatrics.

"Shit! This just became a hostage rescue mission," Declan said.

"If this is the guy that got the drop on Nick, then we'd better be on our toes," Izzy said.

"We've got an advantage," Declan said confidently.

"Yeah, what's that?" Izzy asked.

"He doesn't know that we can track her. We can follow from a distance, and then when they stop, we make our move."

Izzy registered that Declan's face held an air of contentedness. The thought of conflict seemed to bring with it a sense of peace. A strange genetic make-up to this battle-hardened man. Her heart raced at the thought of this potential standoff.

Declan smiled and said, "Don't worry, Izzy. We've got this."

Nodding, she pushed the pedal and accelerated the Camry as Declan kept a watchful eye on the red dot labeled MX1249.

Chapter 49

He punched the message into the phone as he drove. His large fingers nimbly navigated the screen, while maintaining a steady focus on the road ahead. The storm that had helped mask his attack on the lawman subsided quickly. Steam rose from the hot asphalt, and the dense humidity caused him to use the wipers intermittently. The message he sent was simple and clear: *She's with me.*

Cain waited for the response, driving south. He didn't know how the Pastor would like him to proceed with the Heathen, but he knew it was best to begin the long journey back to Texas. His phone alerted to the incoming message, and he looked at the response: *Relax Inn just across the border into Arkansas. Room 117. Key's at the desk. Someone will be there to meet you.*

Cain tried to interpret the meaning. *Did he fail again? Why would the Pastor send someone else to finish the task at the bus depot? Was he being replaced?*

He squeezed at his massive thigh and could feel the wound re-open. The pain provided little in the way of relief to his sudden frustration. He pressed play on the Ford's center console, looking to find solace in the Pastor's words.

As if the recordings were preset to Cain's current circumstance, the Pastor rang out his wisdom.

It is not for you to know. It is not for you to control. The direction God gives you in life is known only to him. I've been lucky enough to be a vessel to share his wisdom. To speak his commands. To guide the lost. Believe in me. Trust in my words. You shall walk in the light and carry forth on a just and righteous path.

Cain released his leg. Entering the GPS coordinates to his new destination, he was overcome with a feeling of excitement. Almost giddy, he wondered if the Pastor would be there to greet him. It'd been so long since he'd last been in his presence. The wishful thought carried him forward into the night.

The Heathen whimpered behind him, and Cain turned up the volume to drown out the sound. It wouldn't be long until he would complete his task and reap the reward. The praise he so desperately sought.

Cain retrieved the key from the main desk and went back to the vehicle. The CD played and continued to blare the sermon. This was done to drown out any attempted cries for help that the Heathen may attempt while he was inside. He returned and looked down at the girl on the floorboard. She hadn't moved. He reached his hand down under the heavy blanket, running his finger along her neck in search of a pulse. Still alive, he drove around to the rear of the motel and parked in front of room 117.

The backside of the motel was L-shaped. There was nothing to the rear of the structure, except a dilapidated fenced-in area that protected a filled pool. Weeds had broken through the concrete in several places, reaching out from the ground and up the expanse of the fence. The Relax Inn appeared to be anything but. It was definitely a long-forgotten waypoint for weary travelers. Perfect for meetings like this. Perfect for a Heathen's end.

It was deserted, except for one light green sedan parked in a nearby spot. Cain assumed this vehicle belonged to the person he was set to meet. Not sure who or why this meeting was to take place, but he followed the Pastor's instructions blindly, trusting in the man who had given him his life meaning.

Cain lowered the volume on the car stereo. Leaving the Heathen on the floorboard, he stepped from the Ford. His foot landed in a puddle of warm water, a remnant from the recent storm. The water soaked into his shoes, causing them to squeak slightly as he shuffled slowly to the door. The gait of his step was off-kilter, favoring his injured thigh.

The flat plastic electronic key slipped into the slot and a click sounded, indicating that the door was now unlocked. In the stillness of the humid night air, Cain heard the creak of a chair.

Cain slipped the pistol from the holster on his hip. The weapon looked like a child's toy in his large hand. He held it behind his back as he pushed the handle and opened the door, exposing himself to the room's occupant.

He entered without saying a word as the door closed behind him.

Chapter 50

"Nick said they've got some local support coming. Maybe we should wait. Let them handle it," Izzy said, wavering in her usual confidence.

"Not a chance! This asshole tried to end our friend, killed a goddamned trooper, and abducted a little girl," Declan said, intensely.

The focus in his eyes told the remainder. He was in operational mode, and Izzy knew that any further attempts to sway him would be futile. She drew her compact Glock 23 from the inside-the-waistband holster on the small of her back.

"You go, I go," Izzy said, declaring her trust in the man seated in the passenger seat.

Their Camry remained parked in front of the Relax Inn's main entrance. Izzy and Declan stepped inside the meager management office. The smell of burnt coffee and cigarettes wafted as they entered. The two flashed their credentials to the clerk. His eyes widened and he wiped his nose on his sleeve, leaning in to inspect the badges.

"What can I do ya fer?" The clerk said, straightening his posture in an attempt to convey some level of professionalism.

"How long has he been in there?" Declan asked.

"Um, which one?" The clerk said, scratching at a scab on his arm.

"What do you mean which one?" Izzy said, jumping in the conversation.

"Well, ya' see there is two of 'em. One came in a few minutes b'fer the other," the clerk said, his eyes bouncing between the two agents standing before him.

"Okay, so how long?" Declan asked again.

"Dunno. Maybe fifteen. Nah, prob-b-b-bly two-wen-n-t-ty," the clerk said, taking on a nervous stammer.

"Thank you," Izzy said, realizing that the clerk was overwhelmed by the situation. "How about you sketch me the layout of the room?"

Satisfied by the crude drawing of Room 117's schematic, the two agents departed the clerks' office with the duplicate key that he'd made. In the muggy night air, the two moved on foot toward the room. Declan made one last check of the image on his phone's screen.

"Still there. No movement."

Izzy let out a long, controlled breath. The tension in her face was only equaled by the strength in her dark eyes.

"You pop the door, and I'm going to push the room. It's going to be tight. Just be on my ass when I enter," Declan said, pitching the plan on the fly.

"I've got your six," Izzy said confidently.

"Never doubted that," Declan whispered.

Declan raised his balled fist up by his ear, halting his progression. The silent gesture stopped Izzy. They made eye contact and Declan pointed ahead, indicating that they were approaching the target location. Izzy nodded and they proceeded at a much slower pace as they closed the distance to the room.

Declan stopped again and then pointed at the door. Without saying a word, Izzy came around to the front of their two-person assault team. Izzy held the electronic key at the ready, scanning the rooms exterior. The drapes were drawn, and the lights were off. She inhaled deeply and let the tension out with a long breath.

Declan held his pistol at the low-ready. He stood behind Izzy and reached up with his left hand. Squeezing her shoulder, he gave Izzy the signal to initiate, and she pushed the key into the metal slot. The click seemed as loud as a hammer on a nail. She pushed down on the handle, opening the door. Izzy moved to the right, allowing Declan a clear path into the room. His body was a blur of movement as he shot past her. She'd forgotten how fast he moved and lunged into the room to keep up.

"Hands! Now!" Declan boomed at the man seated in the chair facing the door.

The large man sat in the dark and didn't move.

Declan stepped closer, but in the dark, it was difficult to make out the silent man's features.

"Don't move!" Declan then spoke over his shoulder to Izzy and said, "Hit the lights."

Izzy turned to flick the light switch.

The door slammed shut, and what little light that was provided from the outside moonlight disappeared. The room was cast into darkness.

"Shit!" Izzy yelled.

Declan spun, and Izzy's head smacked him hard on the side of his, like two coconuts clacking together. The impact sent him staggering backward, and he tripped over the seated man's leg, falling to the not-so-soft carpet.

Looking up from the floor, Declan registered that the seated man was dead or least unconscious. His face was blood covered. Declan scrambled back, scooting along the floor on his butt like a crab. He needed distance from whoever closed that door and tossed Izzy like a rag doll.

Izzy was on the ground and not moving. In the darkness, a large figure had already closed the gap. His frame could have been that of a bear. The speed of the large man was impressive. More so was the impact that his fist carried as it came crashing down on Declan's eye. Dizzied by the blow, Declan fired his gun blindly at the mountain of a man that hunched over him. He only managed to get one round off before the weight of the large man spilled over him.

Declan couldn't see out his left eye, and his gun hand was now pinned to the floor by a knee. It might as well have been sealed in concrete as Declan struggled in vain to pull free. More punches rained down, but this time, they peppered his body as well. It was like being hit with a sledgehammer. Declan had been in plenty of hand-to-hand battles, but he'd never been so overwhelmed.

The man then pressed both of his large hands around Declan's neck and squeezed. The flow of oxygen was cut off, and Declan writhed to fight his way out. The room was getting darker, and sounds began to fade. The bald man's face got closer as he applied more pressure.

His eyes were a scary calm. The bald man watched curiously as Declan felt his life slipping away. Sweat rolled down the madman's face and onto his. Wheezing, he thrashed in agony. In that moment of utter desperation, he saw his girls. He pictured each one's face as the world around him blurred.

The bald man's eyes flashed in a combination of shock and anger as his head snapped forward. Izzy wrapped tightly around his neck like a boa constrictor. She clawed at his face. The bald man tried to ignore the interruption and was intent on finishing his work with Declan, but she was relentless.

He loosened his grip, launching upright. He stood with Izzy on his back. She looked like a child receiving a piggyback ride. If not for the dire circumstances, it would have been almost comical.

Declan forced himself into a fast, if not temporary, recovery and tried to take aim on the Man Mountain that stood above him. Izzy's back now provided a shield, leaving him no clear shot. Declan aimed low and fired at the big man's legs. With his vision still blurred from the damaging blows, Declan concentrated hard to aim his shots and the rounds found their mark.

The pain of the gunshots caused him to spasm, flinging Izzy over the bed. She came crashing down onto an end table. He collapsed to his hands and knees, holding the fresh wounds to his calves. Even kneeling, the man was enormous. The bloodied behemoth spun towards Declan, a ravenous look filled his eyes.

What little ambient light existed in the room was washed away as the large man launched toward him. Declan aimed for center mass and squeezed the trigger.

The muzzle flash in the darkness was blinding. Declan continued to send rounds at the target until the mountain toppled. The dead weight of the man slammed down on Declan.

Declan wheezed as he pushed hard, sliding out from under. He climbed atop the man's back that was now slick with the blood emptying from the exit wounds. He roughly grabbed the beast's neck and searched for a pulse. Nothing.

Declan then crawled his way to Izzy, who was lying face down in a pile of broken wood and glass. He touched her arm, and she spun, swinging wildly. Declan caught her arm by the wrist.

"It's me! He's down," Declan said reassuringly.

"Sorry," Izzy said, cautiously. "You sure?"

"I hope so 'cause I'm out of bullets," Declan said, returning to his calm, almost cocky, demeanor.

The tension in her muscles went slack and the two slumped against the cheap box spring of the bed.

"The girl!" Izzy yelled. Panic filled her eyes.

"Bathroom!" Declan said, pushing himself up from the ground.

Izzy flicked on the lights. A macabre scene set before them. The large bodies of the two dead men occupied much of the small room. As much as Declan and Izzy wanted to rush into the bathroom, part of them was terrified at what they might find.

Declan opened the door to the bathroom and saw the dark blanket covering a small body in the bathtub. His heart sank. He'd always been able to distance himself from the horrors of the world, but in this moment, he failed to do so. He couldn't shake the thought of his own daughters from his mind. The taste of bile filled his mouth and he leaned against the sink.

"Mouse! It's us. The two from the bus station. Friends of Nick and Anaya," Izzy said, hoping for some response.

Nothing.

Izzy closed the distance to the little girl. Collecting herself, she pulled back the shroud to reveal the delicate features of the small girl. She seemed even smaller now.

Declan stood watching from the doorway, a sickening sadness filling him.

"Mouse?" Izzy whispered.

Nothing.

Izzy bent low and gently pressed two fingers along the child's exposed neckline.

Mouse's eyelids fluttered. She opened them slowly as if waking from a terrible nightmare.

"Oh, thank God!" Izzy scooped the small teenager from the tub and brought her to the bed. Declan pulled a Gerber multi-tool from his waist and clipped the zip ties, freeing the girl's hands.

Without warning, Mouse shot her arms out, wrapping them tightly around Izzy's neck. She buried her head in Izzy's shoulder and wept softly. Izzy held her for what seemed like an eternity.

The embrace was interrupted by the sound of police radios as members of the Arkansas State Police filled the room.

Chapter 51

After working things out with state police, the three departed for Austin. The drive back was uneventful. Izzy drove the entire way because Declan's left eye was completely closed. Mouse slept soundly, only waking once. When the weary trio arrived, they were greeted by Nick, who was in the company of Kemper Jones and Anaya Patel.

Jones saw the exhaustion on Izzy's face and offered her a quiet office in the back that had long ago been converted into a bedroom. It'd proven necessary too many times to count when a big case rolled in. Izzy didn't protest the offer and followed him back.

Declan and Nick exchanged smiles as the two men took stock of each other's injuries. Anaya squatted down and looked at Mouse. She put out her hand toward the teen. Mouse only hesitated for a moment before taking it.

"I'm going to talk with her for a moment and let you two boys catch up," Anaya said, walking away hand in hand with Mouse.

"You look like you went a couple rounds with Mike Tyson," Nick said with a chuckle.

"You should see the other guy," Declan retorted.

Both men grabbed at their aching sides as they laughed. The last twenty-four hours had taken its toll on the two hardened men.

"I can't thank you enough for what you and Izzy did for me, for Mouse," Nick said. His tone was serious now.

"No thanks needed. I'm going to be on a little vacation when I get back to Connecticut, while the bureau waits for the all-clear from the Arkansas State Police on my shooting," Declan said.

"That's nothing you can't handle. You've been through worse," Nick said.

Nick broke eye contact and looked down. He pursed his lips and let out a shallow breath that escaped between his clenched teeth, making a quiet hiss. Declan noticed that Nick wanted to say something else but was holding back.

"What is it?" Declan asked, prodding Nick.

"Doesn't matter. It's in the past," Nick said, still avoiding eye contact with his friend.

"No time like the present. Spit it out," Declan said.

"It's just something that's been eating at me a bit," Nick said, again stopping himself.

"There's nothing you can't say to me. Not now. Not ever," Declan said.

"The money from the bank job. What happened to the money?" Nick asked sheepishly.

"You mean the buried treasure?" Declan smiled but continued before Nick could speak. "It bothered me too. Once I was cleared and the FBI gave me the opportunity with HRT, I didn't want the money. But I couldn't give it back either."

"So what'd you do?" Nick asked, looking around to ensure that nosy ears weren't listening.

"Val and I talked. We'd spent some of it to get back on our feet before the Khaled thing blew up. Literally. But we decided that I should try to do something good with the money left over." Declan sighed and continued, "Even though the Jamal Anderson shooting was ruled as justified, I was devastated when I learned he'd been a pawn in Khaled's twisted game. So, I decided to try to make it right as best I could. I found the mother of his infant child, and after doing a little bit of research into her life, I learned that she was a waitress working double shifts to provide a good life for her son. I had an attorney draft up a non-disclosure benefactor contract, and a week later, Shakira Anderson received a $60,000 check."

"Jesus. That's a weight off my shoulders," Nick said. He put a hand on his friend's shoulder and leaned closer. "You did the right thing."

"I hope so, but the weight of Jamal's death isn't going anywhere. It's something I'm going to have to carry with me to the grave," Declan said seriously.

Jones walked up to the two men and saw that they were engaged in a deep conversation.

"Not to interrupt, but I got the strangest update from the Homicide Unit of the Arkansas State Police," Jones said, shaking his head in disbelief. "That big guy that y'all went toe-to-toe with had one of them damn microchips in his hip. Been in there awhile they said. Branded too."

"Do you think he started off like Mouse?" Declan asked, unfamiliar with these types of investigations.

"Anything's possible. Could've been taken and abused. Maybe they saw some potential use for him outside of the trade. The brainwashing by these organizations is legendary," Nick responded, thoughtfully.

"Well, whatever humanity he'd been born with had been torn out of him. He died a monster," Declan said, rubbing his damaged eye.

"True. I've arranged with the hospital to have the tracking device removed from Mouse's hip. We don't need any more surprise visitors showing up," Jones said to the pair, changing the subject.

Everybody nodded in agreement.

Anaya returned with Mouse in tow. She had her arm draped loosely over the small teenagers shoulder in a nonchalant half-hug. Standing there side by side they could have been mother and daughter.

"She understands. No more running." Anaya looked down at Mouse, who gave a weak smile. It was the first time any of them had seen her show this emotion, and it lifted the group's tension slightly.

"Where were you going to run to?" Nick asked, looking down at Mouse.

"Pidgeon," Mouse said quietly.

"Pidgeon?" Nick asked, thoroughly confused by the teen's remark.

"Pidgeon, Michigan," Mouse spoke confidently as if this would explain everything to the four adults standing around her.

"Why there? Family?" Nick asked.

"No."

Mouse paused and looked down at her feet. She swayed from side to side with her hands clasp in front. Under the child's tough exterior Nick saw that she was still just a little girl. She looked up with a cheeky grin.

Feeling comfortable with her saviors, Mouse explained, "I wanted to get as far away from here as I could. I grabbed a map and pushed my finger up until I hit blue."

"But I still don't understand why you chose Pidgeon," Nick said.

"It sounded like a fun place to start my new life," Mouse's said, broadening her smile.

"Makes sense to me," Declan said. "I think that we should find a way to get you there."

"I'm already working on it," Anaya said, smiling down at Mouse.

The group laughed, the four adults thoroughly impressed at the resilience of the little girl standing before them.

Chapter 52

"What do you mean they went dark?" Nick asked.

"I mean, as soon as you guys recovered the girl, they must have realized that we figured out the tracking system. They shut it down or, more likely, just reconfigured it so that we couldn't follow the trackers anymore," Jay said.

"Shit! I planned to try to hit as many of those locations as humanly possible. I mean, we could've shut down a major network. We could've saved a lot of kids," Nick said sadly.

Nick slumped in the chair. The injection of pain that radiated from his recovering stab wound was a welcomed distraction to his worry. The phone was still pressed against his ear but Nick said nothing else, lost in his thoughts.

"I may have some good news for you. For starters, I sent the last data points to a group that handles this sort of thing. Non-governmental, but extremely effective. These guys operate outside the system. You might not ever hear the end result. But you can rest assured that they'll be able to help some. The ones they didn't relocate," Jay said.

"Some but not all," Nick interjected softly.

"You know you can't save 'em all." Jay paused, allowing for his friend to absorb the truth of that statement. He continued, "The other good news came from the phone that you took off that guy in the motel. He'd sent a message just before your friends raided the room. It was a picture of the dead guy in the chair and a message that read: *Why have you forsaken me*?"

"Please tell me you know who he sent it to!" Nick exclaimed.

"You won't believe me when I do," Jay said.

The crowd that surrounded the Safe Haven Children's Center's grand opening gala was larger than expected. It was filled with families supporting the launch of the new facility. A beacon of hope aimed at being an outreach to families in need. The project was funded in large part by the charitable donations from God's Reach Ministries.

The podium was occupied by the well-dressed Pastor Jim Collins. He looked upon the crowd and smiled widely as cheers erupted from supporters and congregation members. He absorbed the adoration like a beachgoer soaking up the sun. Satisfied, he attempted a gesture of humility, waving his hand in an attempt to subdue the hoots and hollers of his fans.

The roar subsided, and he began his speech.

"It is with a great pleasure that I am called before you today. It looks like the rain will hold off long enough to celebrate this momentous occasion. I'm humbled to be asked to introduce a great man, a man who is not only a close personal friend of mine, but a true believer in the betterment of our society, a man who stands against injustice and seeks to provide shelter to children in need. Senator Duke Murdock has worked tirelessly to bring together the pieces that have made today possible. Without him, I don't think that the Safe Have Children's Center would be a reality."

Collins allowed a pause, so the crowd could cheer and clap. He turned and gave a rehearsed nod to the senator, who was waiting eagerly for his turn in the spotlight.

Collins gaze returned to the onlookers and continued, "My heart is light today. Lifted by the kindness of those who donated their time and money to this project. I look out into this crowd and see so many who will benefit from the services that will be provided within these walls. So many of our young children are swallowed up by the streets, by people with evil in their hearts, tearing them from their families. I am committed to finding these lost souls and giving them refuge. I am committed to pushing back against the beast and providing safety. I will not rest until all children are safe!"

The crowd exploded in a contagious volley of cheers. This time, Collins allowed it to continue. He looked back again, smiling in the direction of the senator. The smile drained from the pastor's face as he saw a group of men and women in the clearly recognizable blue windbreakers. The jackets adorned with the distinctive bright yellow lettering, FBI.

The senator's back was turned and he was already leaving the stage. Senator Murdock, encircled by his protective detail, disappeared into the heavily tinted black Suburban, never looking back to see the fate of the man on the podium.

Dumbfounded. For the first time in his adult life, he was at a total loss for words. Pastor Jim Collins swung his head wildly from the approaching agents to the hushed crowd as if debating on leaping from the stage. The cool-headedness of the charismatic evangelist was gone. What remained was a terrified shell of a man.

He fumbled with the words, trying to play it off as some type of misunderstanding. The microphone still on and capturing his desperation.

"What can I help you gentlemen with today? Can't you see that we're in the middle of an important ceremony? It's for the children!" Collins pleaded.

"Children are the last thing you're here for!" Nick said, barely keeping his cool.

Nick walked slowly toward the religious figurehead. His hand rested on the butt of his service weapon. It was still holstered but poised to react if the need arose.

"Put your hands behind your back."

"I don't understand," Collins protested.

"Would you like me to explain the charges to the crowd?" Nick asked through gritted teeth.

"You're going to hear from my lawyers on this!" Collins said in a last-ditch effort to save face.

Nick's hand slid from the gun to his handcuff case, retrieving the stainless steel Smith and Wesson cuffs. The pastor stood rigid, more out of shock than defiance. Nick reached out and gripped Collins at the elbow, spinning him around.

Nick winced slightly as he locked the cuffs into place on the pastor. The interim week since his stabbing hadn't left him fit for duty, but he'd be damned if he was going to miss an opportunity to make this arrest. He handed Pastor Jim Collins off to the agent who'd be transporting and processing him.

Collins was walked off the same stage he'd been so wildly welcomed to moments before. Not a sound from his adoring fans could be heard as he was placed into the rear of a blacked-out bureau SUV.

Before the door shut Nick leaned in and whispered in the pastor's ear, "I was really hoping you would've resisted a little."

Nick turned and saw his ragtag group of friends standing by. Declan's eye was healing, but he still looked like he'd been hit by a bus. Rusty and Jones stood in the backdrop with a satisfied look on their faces as they watched Collins get hauled away.

It was a surreal moment for Nick to see Izzy and Anaya side by side. Both beautiful women. One lost to him and the other an unknown. Izzy smiled coyly and then shot a questioning glance at the social worker. Nick flushed at the realization that Izzy must've caught him sizing up the two.

Jones rubbed his belly and said in a thick Texas drawl, "Let's get some grub. I've got just the spot for these Yankees. Y'all ever had brisket?"

The group laughed, and Declan said, "I'd love to, but we've got to make the ride. I've got to get back to my little ones. Raincheck on that."

The group started to separate, and Nick walked with Declan and Izzy over to their rental car.

Declan and Nick shook hands, gave the "man hug" followed by a slap on the back. Each regretted the gesture as soon as the hearty embrace ended. Their injuries throbbed, reminding them of the toll their bodies had taken.

"You think hard about coming back to Connecticut, my friend. If you can manage to keep from getting injured, I might be able to get you a slot on HRT!" Declan said.

"I think my place is here, at least for now," Nick said.

"We're here for you whenever you need," Declan paused and then added, "I'll let you kids talk."

Declan slipped into the passenger seat of the Camry and closed the door.

"He's right you know," Izzy said softly.

"Right about what?"

"About being here for you," Izzy said, looking into his eyes.

"Same here," Nick said and then faltered at saying anything more.

"You're a stubborn ass, Nicholas Lawrence! Do you know that?" Izzy said.

"So I've heard." Nick looked at his former partner and sighed.

He didn't know the words to say, so he said nothing. He pulled Izzy close and held her. The smell of coconut and vanilla filled the air as her head lay gently over his shoulder. After a short embrace, she retracted, sliding her hands down his arms until their fingertips touched. She looked at him intently, leaned in, and pressed her lips against his cheek and then broke away. She opened the driver's door and looked up at him as she entered the car, her eyes watering.

"Don't' go getting yourself killed! There're a lot of people that care about you," Izzy said, closing the door behind her.

The Camry drove off. Nick looked back toward his black Jetta and saw Anaya leaning against the trunk in a golden sundress that flapped effortlessly in the late afternoon breeze. Nick smiled as he walked in her direction, wondering where this might lead.

Be on the lookout for Book 3 in the Nick Lawrence Series:

The Rabbit's Hole

Available November 23rd, 2018

www.brianchristophershea.com

Thank you for reading!

Made in the USA
Middletown, DE
23 August 2018